Millie in the Mirror
The City Under Seattle
Book 2

Thea Thomas
&
Blythe Ayne

Millie in the Mirror
The City Under Seattle
Book 2

Thea Thomas
&
Blythe Ayne

Millie in the Mirror
The City Under Seattle – Book 2
Thea Thomas & Blythe Ayne

Emerson & Tilman, Publishers
129 Pendleton Way #55
Washougal, WA 98671

Millie in the Mirror

ebook ISBN: 978-1-947151-90-1
Paperback ISBN: 978-1-947151-91-8
Large Print ISBN: 978-1-957272-41-2
Hardbound ISBN: 978-1-957272-31-3
Audiobook ISBN: 978-1-957272-32-0

[1. YOUNG ADULT FICTION/Paranormal, Occult & Supernatural
2. YOUNG ADULT FICTION/Romance/Contemporary
3. FICTION/Fantasy/Urban] I. Title.
BIC: FM

DEDICATION

*To Those Who Treasure
Their Friendships Above All*

Books by Thea Thomas

Contemporary Sweet Romance:
Canyon Road
One Love
Two Weddings
Three Proposals

Books by Thea Thomas &
Blythe Ayne
Young Adult:
The People in the Mirror
Millie in the Mirror
The Angel in the Mirror

Paranormal Romance:
Amethyst Dream
Porcelain Claws

Table of Contents

Chapter I from: Angel in the Mirror

Chapter 1
Not Great News

"I've got great news," Dad announced at dinner.

I felt caution rise up my spine. Dad's "great news" often meant something I would *not* name "great news."

"What's that, dear?" Mom asked. I sensed the same caution from her.

"I have to go back down to Orange County for a few weeks on my job. And now that school's almost out for the summer, we can all be at home for the summer. Of course, we can't stay in our house as it's sublet, but I'll rent a nice little place. Won't that be great! What do you say, Nikki? Summer in Laguna Beach? Great, yes?" He could not have smiled bigger, so pleased with himself.

"Ahh, no, Dad. Not really." How could he not know that I've been looking forward to school getting out with every fiber of my being? Because, one, I'll be able to spend more time with Mitch, and two, my friend Yumi was coming to stay with me for the summer. We've been planning it for *three months*, and I've been babbling on about it, like, *forever*. Where does Dad go when I talk?

Mom glanced at me. There was something in her look that made me even more anxious. "Oh dear," she said.

Dad looked from me to Mom, and from Mom to me. "What am I missing?"

"Quite a lot, Dad. Have you not heard me planning and planning and planning on Yumi coming to stay the summer? … And …."

"Well, yes, I've heard that, yes. But I thought if you were there, that would be altogether better. See?"

"No, Dad. No. The whole point … I mean … *hmmmm*, if you don't just 'get it' I can't explain it."

Dad shook his head. "I don't get it."

"Well, my dear, there's Mitch," Mom chimed in. "Nikki's looking forward to sharing her life here with her friend, Yumi, and there's Mitch."

"Well, yes," Dad nodded, "Of course, Mitch, I know, there's Mitch. But I thought you'd be so happy to go home for a few weeks. I thought you could stand to be away from Mitch for a while." Dad paused. "*But!*" He lit up like he'd created a brilliant invention. "How about this? Mitch can come down and visit us for a few days, and you could show him Laguna Beach. Now, *there's* a plan!"

I couldn't be mad at him. He was trying. But he still missed the point that my friends and I had been making plans for *weeks*.

"Well," Mom interceded, "that's sweet, dear, although Nikki and her friends have been making a lot of plans for some while. But," and she gave me that apologetic look again, "and I'm sorry, Nikki—I was about to make an announcement at dinner myself. My school called today and begged me to come down and teach in their new summer program for children at risk.

"Well, I jumped at the opportunity! It's an eight-week program, and it's exactly the work that's so meaningful to me." Mom juiced up the apologetic look. "What a strange coincidence, that we both have summer jobs in O.C.!" Mom reached across the table and patted my hand. "I'm sorry, sweetie, to upset your plans, but it looks like we'll all be heading south for the summer."

I looked at Mom, dismayed. "*Ahhhhh ....*" I couldn't add any actual words to my dismay.

"I know, Nikki, it's upsetting, but your dad has a pretty good plan, off the cuff like that. Have Mitch come down and stay with us for a few days."

"But ... we were going to go to MoPop and the aquarium, we were going to hang out with Alex, we were going to ... oh, so many things!"

I turned my head to look out at the fog hugging the windows like a big soft gray cat, the cozy fog that at first I hated—and had come to love. "Yumi already bought her ticket. She skimped like crazy to get it, and I even gave her some of my allowance. She's coming *day after tomorrow*. Why aren't my plans important? Why can't I just stay here?"

Mom and Dad exchanged a look that said lots, but what, exactly, I could not discern. I plowed on. "First of all, I'm not a little kid anymore, and second, there's Mitch's mom, and there's Homer that I can go to if I need to. And Mr. Zingas, too." I *loved* Alex's dad.

There was that look between Mom and Dad again!

"What I don't get," Dad said, his brow wrinkled, apparently taking in new information, "what I don't get is how all this is going on around me, and I miss it. I thought it was your heart's desire, Nikki, to be home. I thought this would warm the little cockles of your heart."

"Dad, I'm fifteen, almost sixteen, my cockle's desires don't just sit around being the same, day in and day out. Things change. I change. You brought me here, I found friends, and ... and I have a special friend, and now ... I'm happy here."

"And now you're happy here," he repeated, as if learning a new language.

"I … I suppose I could tell them I'm not available for the summer program after all," Mom said in a small, disappointed voice.

"*No!*" Dad and I practically shouted in unison.

"No, Mom, no. Those kids need you," I insisted, thinking quickly how awful it would be if Mom stayed here, instead of getting involved in a program for at-risk kids. It would likely trigger her occasional depression—and because of me. *Not an option.*

But I wasn't willing to simply give up. "How about a compromise. After Yumi gets here and you two go off to Orange County, let us have a week 'test run.' If things don't go smoothly, then Yumi and I will come down to O.C. at the end of that week."

The eye-language between Mom and Dad again, then Dad nodded. "Okay, my little Pumpkin Patch, we'll give you a few days to prove yourself."

I grinned. When he starts calling me his silly "terms of endearment," I know we're on the right track.

"Daily FaceTime," Mom added. "And *no hesitation* from you if there's any problem."

"A fair contract," I said in my best lawyer-y voice. "Where do I sign?"

"Don't get cocky," Dad advised.

I nodded, trying to put on a sober expression. But my grin threatened to eat my face. What a fantastic outcome—my best friend, Yumi, and me, alone in the gorgeous apartment. Young adults on our own!

And, P.S., Mitch next door.

Nothing could go wrong.

Chapter 11
Best Friends

So two days later we drove to the airport to pick up Yumi and drop off Dad.

It worked out perfectly—we first got Yumi and had a nice little lunch together, then waved goodbye to Dad as he scurried to his flight. Mom would leave the following Monday, taking a Lyft to the airport. I knew it suited her to be sure that Yumi was all settled in. And, well, to simply feel safe to leave the two of us young miscreants to our own devices.

I was *soooo* happy to see Yumi! All we'd shared as best friends since we were little girls came tumbling out the moment we hugged.

"*I missed you!*" she exclaimed in her delicate voice, lightly laced with the hint of Japanese, her first language.

"Me too you! Look at you! More beautiful than ever. How do you do that?"

"Oh!" She tittered softly and looked down shyly. "No, no I'm not. But you are! Something here is very good for you!"

"It's the endless mist. Makes me dewy." I wasn't serious, of course. Just babbling, so delighted to see her.

Dad wrangled us into a restaurant. I was so excited, I could hardly eat, but managed to get down a bowl of soup. The chatter at the table was pleasant but entirely superficial. There was something about Yumi I couldn't put my finger on. She wasn't quite herself.

Was she cautious about being here? Was she, suddenly shy? Had something happened to her that I didn't know about?

As it turned out, I was right on all three points, which would come out over the next few days.

On the drive back to the apartment, Yumi and I sat in the back seat with Mom as our chauffeur. I asked Yumi a raft of questions. She responded with a soft "yes" or "no," or simply shrugged. I had to accept that she just did not want to talk yet. Maybe not in range of Mom's hearing. Maybe not at all. I wasn't sure, but I was sure she was blocking my efforts at a real conversation.

"It's raining," she observed as Mom drove out of the airport and onto the freeway.

"True," I agreed. "That's Seattle. If it's not misting, it's raining. I think I kinda mentioned that." Yeah, like, at first, every day I texted her, "It's misting," "It's raining." Then I got used to it, and stopped with the weather reports.

"I thought," Yumi said, mind-reading, "when you stopped saying every day that it was misting or raining, it had stopped."

Mom and I burst out laughing. "Oh, no! I just got used to it. And I figured, mercifully for you, no doubt, that you didn't need to read that it was doing the same thing that it does every day."

"Oh. *Hmmm.*" Yumi fell silent. Did the rain bother her that much? I certainly hoped not.

"Home again," I chirped as Mom drove into our parking structure.

"*Wow!*" Yumi looked up at the gargoyles on the building, "*Protectors!*"

"I guess so," I said, surprised at her observation and even more surprised that she seemed happier to see the gargoyles than to see me. "I never thought of them that way… but of course they're our protectors." We climbed out of the car, gathered Yumi's luggage and backpack from the trunk, then headed for the back entrance to the elevators.

When we stepped inside the back entrance, Homer, the doorman, came up to us while we waited for the elevator. "This must be your charming guest," he tipped his hat ever so slightly.

"Yes, Homer. This is Yumi," Mom said, "Nikki's friend since they were little girls. Yumi, this is Homer, our kindly doorman."

Yumi bowed her head, "Nice to meet you, sir."

"Call me Homer, please."

"All right," Yumi agreed, eyes still averted.

I exchanged a look with Mom over Yumi's head. She was generally quiet and polite, but this was *strange.*

The elevator dinged and the doors slid open. We rode up in silence. When the doors opened on the seventh floor and we stepped into the lovely pale peach light, Yumi sighed audibly.

"What lovely light," she exclaimed.

"I know. I love it," I agreed, relieved to hear a hint of her usual enthusiasm.

We walked down the hall to our apartment, silent footfalls in the dense carpet. Mom unlocked the door and we stepped inside, where the cozy warmth of the apartment embraced us.

"Oh!" Yumi exclaimed, taking in the baby grand, the pale green and apricot facing sofas, the rich walnut of the furniture. *"So beautiful!"*

"I'm glad you like it!" I smiled at her, but she still refused to make eye contact. At a loss, I forged ahead, "Let's get you settled in your room, and then I think Mom made some cookies for us this morning, if I'm not mistaken."

"I did," Mom affirmed, moving toward the piano. "If you don't mind, I'd like to play for a bit while you girls get settled, as I'm soon to leave this glorious piano."

I felt certain that Mom was leaving the two of us alone so I could get to the heart of what was bothering Yumi, and I was grateful for her wordless understanding.

Yumi and I walked down the hall to her guest room. I'd spent a good chunk of my allowance, and hours and hours of my time, putting up posters of her favorite Japanese anime artists that, frankly, I knew very little about. She aspired to become one herself, and if anyone could, it'd be Yumi. Super-talented, she'd already produced a couple of beautiful comics, and even had a small-but-loyal following on the internet.

As the rich tones of Beethoven flowed around us, Yumi took in the posters with a grin. "You put up anime artists just for me in your room?"

"I put up anime artists just for you in your room. This is your very own room. Mine is across the hall," I gestured toward the door.

"*Oh!*" She sounded disappointed.

I had given a lot of thought about sharing my bedroom. Yumi and I had shared my room or her room our whole childhood. But, I thought, if we were living together for several weeks, she'd probably want some space to herself.

But an even more important consideration was my mirror, about which I had two major concerns. The first being, if she saw the people and things in the mirror that I saw on occasion, it would terrify her. The second being, if she never saw anything in the mirror when I did, it would *frighten me!*

"I thought you could use some space to yourself since you're going to be here for a few weeks," I explained. "You like things tidy, and me, well, you know, not so much."

I finally succeeded in making Yumi giggle. "True! Okay, it's good. I love what you've done. Just for me. It's so sweet!" She turned and gave me a hug. "So I guess I get all the drawers and all the closet to myself!"

"Indeed, you do."

I sat on the edge of the bed and watched as she carefully unpacked, deliberately putting each item in a drawer or on hangers in the closet. I knew that I could step into this room at any time, and it would be exactly like this. Neat as a pin.

"Anyway, I'm just across the hall, and my door is always open."

"Yes." Yumi said softly. And again, she seemed to withdraw into some inscrutable place, much more inaccessible to me than my room across the hall.

"How about those cookies?" I asked after her roller board and backpack were neatly stowed in the closet.

"Of course," Yumi nodded, glancing around the room for one last thing daring to be out of place.

"And a tour of the mansion," I suggested.

"I'd like that. It's very impressive, this apartment up here in the clouds." "Very dramatic, isn't it, this weather?"

"Well, I guess so. Lots of shifting energies, yes. I've always felt it."

Yumi nodded. Then, finally, she came over to me, put her arm around my waist and leaned her head against my shoulder. "Thank you for being my friend."

"Oh, Yumi!" I gave her a big hug. "I've really, *really* missed you!" I felt just a bit like crying, overwhelmed with a rush of emotion, glad that she finally warmed up to me, sad that something deeply bothered her.

Arm in arm, we went back to the living room and sat on the sofa, enjoying Mom's amazing playing. *She* would miss it? *I would miss it,* I just realized.

When she finished the piece she turned to us. "Cookies?"

"Of course! And we're going to take a grand tour of the apartment."

"Good idea," Mom agreed. "First let's tour, then we'll hunker down in the kitchen with our warm cookies and tea."

We ambled back down the hall, starting at the far end of the apartment with my room. It was in its usual jumble of a few items of clothing on the bed, and a couple of stacks of books lying about. Not at all bad.

"Goodness, Nikki, your room is as big as an apartment," Yumi exclaimed. "Lots of space to clutter, but it's pretty neat."

"Thanks … probably just a bit in your honor, I pulled it together." As I showed her my giant closet, I flipped on the bright light I'd asked the workers to install when they sheet rocked the wall between my closet and Mitch's uncle's closet. I'd learned that bright light made anything appearing in my mystical mirror invisible.

Then we went into Mom and Dad's room, even bigger than mine, and tastefully luxurious. Of course, it was neat as a pin too, making it seem more likely that Yumi was related to Mom than I.

After appreciating *"The Inner Sanctum"* as I referred to their room, we walked through the living room, and down the hall adjacent to the kitchen, stepping into the beautiful, formal dining room, with a huge vintage walnut table and ten chairs. We almost never ate in here – it was a bit too formal, and the table too-too big for our casual dining.

"Beautiful room!" Yumi exclaimed.

"It is, although we rarely come in here. *Too big!*" Yumi nodded.

Then we stepped back out into the hall and went into the absolutely breath-taking, plant and Art Nouveau statuary-filled, conservatory.

"Oh! *Ohhhhhh!*" Yumi gasped. She studied the spacious room then looked at me incredulously. "You told me you had a room with plants in it. You didn't tell me it was like this – it's an enchanted forest!" She wandered among the exotic plants, eyes wide in wonder.

I trailed along after her, while Mom stood in the doorway. "Well, I didn't say much because, partly, it's hard to describe," I said, "and, partly, I wanted to surprise you when you came. I was sure you'd love it."

Mom joined us as we meandered on the little wandering stone path to the two walls of windows. Looking out, there was nothing to see but the darkening fog.

Yumi turned back to face the room. "I could … I could sleep in here. I would be perfectly happy with a sleeping bag, right here on the floor."

Mom and I exchanged a glance.

"There's a rollaway bed in the hall closet, Yumi. You're welcome to set it up in here if you wish," Mom said. "Honestly, that's a fantastic idea. I've never thought of it."

"Really? I really can do that?"

"If you wish," Mom affirmed. "By the way, Nikki, please do not neglect the plants when I'm gone, you know they need their watering and feeding."

"I'll take care of them, Mom, don't worry."

"That's the one thing the Rionews begged us to do—please take care of the plants."

"The Rionews?" Yumi asked, wandering back among the plants.

"The people we're sub-letting this apartment from," Mom said. "Mr. Rionews works for the same company as Nikki's dad, and he's on a job in England for a year. We were very fortunate to be able to lease this beautiful place for the time being."

"You certainly are! Please let me help Nikki take care of the plants."

"Of course, Yumi, if you'd like."

"I would very much like."

Finally, we made our way back to the kitchen. Mom set out the cookies and put water on for tea, and soon we were munching on delicious fresh cookies filled to the brim with chocolate chips and sipping tea, while Mom read aloud the four pages of "Plant Care" the Rionews had left for us.

I felt myself experiencing an emotion I didn't like. I'd gone from thinking it best if Yumi and I each had a bedroom across the hall from one another, to being strangely disappointed that she wanted to sleep in the plant room, at the *complete opposite end of the apartment.*

You are very silly, I said silently to myself, watching Yumi's enthusiasm as she and Mom pored over the plant document. But my self-reprimand did not dissuade the niggling emotion one little bit.

Chapter III
Good Day, Sunshine

Lost in thought, I hardly even noticed when Yumi and Mom left the kitchen. But when they pulled out the rollaway bed from the hall closet and pushed it, rumbling through the apartment to the conservatory, they finally had my attention. I knew I ought to get up and help them.

But I didn't want to. I indulged myself in a spate of self-involved irritation. I'd told Mitch not to call tonight because I wanted to spend the evening with Yumi. But I was *not* spending the evening with Yumi. I went on in my mind about how I'd put so much time and thought into making her room just the way she'd like it, and then I let myself begrudge the money I'd spent on those posters that meant nothing to me. And, apparently, meant nothing to Yumi, either.

I listened to Mom and Yumi setting up the rollaway among the plants, chattering away gleefully. Then I heard Mom walk back down the hall, I presumed to get more blankets or what-have-you. But a moment later she popped her head into the kitchen, arms filled with blankets. "Aren't you joining us?"

I glanced up at her. "Ahm, not right now."

Mom frowned. "What's … what's the matter?"

"Nothing." I tried to sound like I meant it.

"I … *hmmmm*, I don't quite understand." Then, insightfully, she put two and two together. "Oh. Well … the guest room. Well, dear, this is not about you. Unless, of course, you insist on making it about you."

"No. I know. But I think it needs to be all right if I take a few minutes to adjust to several things. Not just …." I thought about how Yumi had hardly said a word, really, since getting off the plane. How she glanced at the room I worked so hard on. How I had looked forward to spending time with her, and right now, I felt like I didn't know who she was.

And, I realized, maybe I'd made a mistake. Maybe it *would* have been all kinds of better to go with Mom and Dad to O.C. and have Mitch come down and be with me in the lovely, warm, sunny, Laguna Beach summer.

Mom intuited some, at least, of my fleeting, disappointed, thoughts. "Remember, Nikki, if it doesn't work out, you both can come down as soon as your Dad finds a place to live. Which, as you know, he hasn't yet. As it is, I'll be staying with him in a hotel for a few days."

I nodded.

Mom took her arm load of blankets down the hall to the conservatory. And I sat like a big, old, grouchy, lump in the cozy little kitchen nook, studying my cooling mug of tea, wondering where the massive thrill of spending the summer in this apartment, just Yumi and myself, had gone.

*   *

Yumi, delighted with her sleeping arrangement and claiming to be beyond exhausted, soon went to bed on her little rollaway. I didn't even bother to go into the conservatory and look at the arrangement. I just waved at Yumi as she gathered some of her things from the bedroom then scurried to the opposite end of the apartment.

Mom kissed me on the forehead and gave me a hug. "It'll be all right," she said, sounding particularly unconvinced.

I shrugged and went into my room. Contrary to my promise to leave the door open, I closed it with a firm click, then sat on my bed, texting Mitch.

"Not going as I'd planned," I wrote.

He didn't respond. Well, I'd told him I wouldn't be available, and he had plenty to do without being glued to his phone. Sad and lonely, I wandered into my closet to sort out what I'd wear the next day. Mom and had I planned on taking Yumi to the Seattle Waterfront. I stopped in my tracks as a swirling motion grew in the mirror.

Oh no! Not this, too! I couldn't take one more bit of input right now. I tried to make myself step away from the mirror, to turn on the bright light, to leave the closet altogether. But of course, I could not. I watched, mesmerized, as form took place in the mirror. And there, much to my surprise, materialized the image of Millie the Milliner, the billboard in the underground city that Mitch had discovered.

My dismay fell away as I watched, entirely intrigued. Why would she appear to me? Her delicate, beautiful, Victorian features glowed in sepia tones. Then, rising through her features, came the image of a dark, foreboding room. But, even in its darkness, certain details became highlighted, as if being pointed out to me. The detail of the design in the spindles of the wooden archway to the room … then, the location of a window, the glass, apparently, still—and quite surprisingly—intact, showing the ever-present dirt of the subterranean environment on the other side of the window.

The image shifted, with a focus on the floor. My attention was drawn to a small bump in the wooden flooring. Then murky, sepia swirling come over the image, and I was soon looking at the reflection of myself in the mirror, eyebrows raised, bemusement on my features. I continued staring into the mirror for several seconds, but, finally, I shook my head in disbelief, left the closet and returned to my bed.

What … *what* … had I been shown, and *why?* I glanced at my phone. Mitch had responded, "How so?" to my, "Not going as I'd planned." I turned off my phone. I couldn't imagine attempting to communicate with even Mitch right now.

I fell into a fitful sleep.

*   *

I woke in the morning with sunlight filling up my two long, narrow windows, and streaming into the room—unusual enough! – and discovered myself fully clothed.

Shucking yesterday's clothes and moodiness, I jumped into the shower, determined to make a great day of it. *Hey!* There was sunshine and the Seattle Waterfront to explore and my life-long best friend was here.

Weirdly, I completely forgot about the appearance of Millie in the mirror until I stepped into my closet. Then it all came rushing in on me again. I turned out the light, wondering if Millie would make another appearance, but I only saw a dim reflection of me in my bathrobe.

Enough of that! It was time to be in the present moment. Millie's appearance would have to be put on the back burner. I threw on a pair of jeans and a red "I Heart Seattle" tee-shirt. Yeah. I looked like a tourist, but I didn't care. I had come to "heart" Seattle, and I was not ashamed to admit it!

I found myself thinking about how I'd reacted to Yumi when she wanted to sleep in the conservatory last night. *What was the matter with me?* Why did I care? And, in fact, why hadn't I ever thought of it myself? It's a gorgeous space, filled with plants giving off oxygen, and consuming my carbon dioxide. Yumi was *brilliant* for wanting to sleep in the magical space! And I had a nasty, tiny-minded, mean, person I *did not like* in me.

Goodness! Just because Yumi didn't say and do what I had scripted for her I made myself miserable. So, "get over yourself," I exclaimed out loud as I bounced out of my room and down the hall to the conservatory.

But I paused as I neared the glass door. Was Yumi crying? I stepped back and listened closely. Yes, it certainly sounded like it. Oh! I hoped it wasn't because I'd been such a nasty princess. My heart went out to her. I tapped on the glass door and opened it a crack.

"Are you awake?" I whispered.

I heard her stirring, then she replied in a fake-cheery voice. "Just barely!"

I wandered on the path to where Mom and Yumi had set up the little bed. It was altogether charming, with the sunlight and shadows playing on the leaves, spilling over the bed. I sat on the floor beside Yumi and looked up at her, but she kept her head averted.

"Oh, I slept so hard," she said. "I can barely wake up, even in this beautiful sunshine!"

"It's wonderful. I think you must have brought it from Southern California."

Yumi giggled her adorable little giggle. "Yes. I packed it right in my backpack to share with you."

"Good job!" I exclaimed, wrapping my arms around my knees. "Are you ready for a day of adventure?"

"Oh, yes, please," she said with candid enthusiasm. "I'm ready for anything. Your Mom said something about the Seattle Waterfront. It sounds very interesting." She paused and she finally glanced at me. "I like your tee-shirt!"

"We'll have to get you one, and we can be twins."

"Yes. Twins."

We sat in companionable silence for a few minutes, and it was just like when we were little, those pauses when you're smiling inside because you're so comfortable being with your friend in a happy-quiet place.

"There's my girls!" Mom said joining us. "Are we ready to grab some of this delightful sunshine?"

"*Yes!*" Yumi and I chorused together.

"Good! I'll make a bit of breakfast, and we'll be off."

Yumi ambled off to her "other room" to shower and dress, and I went back to text Mitch. He'd added another note to the one of the night before. "I've got some great news. But will wait until I can share it in person. Hope you have a perfect day. Still wondering what didn't go well …."

Now, there's no denying that it's weird to write to the boy you love, as though he's on the other side of the planet, when in fact, he's only on the other side of the wall. I thought of writing that to him, but decided to keep it short. We'd catch up later.

"My dark mood of the evening gone. Happy day in sunshine. I'm off to Seattle Waterfront with Mom & Y. Can't wait to hear your good news! *Hugs & Kisses….*"

I grabbed a jacket and umbrellas because, well, it's Seattle. Then I wolfed down a bowl of cereal while Mom and Yumi ate more delicately—and we were off.

Chapter IV

The Seattle Waterfront

Soon we were battling the sunny-day crowds of locals and tourists at the famed Seattle Waterfront. We went to Pike Place, of course. Yumi found a couple of little souvenir trinkets that caught her fancy, and then, more importantly! we found a clone of my tee-shirt, and we were able to become twins, which Mom said suited her fine as we were easier to spot in the crowded throngs.

After we'd worked our way through the Waterfront, we agreed to come back to the aquarium another day—which I secretly hoped we'd do with Mitch and Alex. We then went to Pioneer Square, lots of charming shops and history. But—and I hadn't known this beforehand—this was where the tour of the underground city started.

I'd kept Mitch's secret about his discovery of the underground city from everyone. After all, it was Mitch's discovery and it was not for me to share it with anyone. Even Mom and Dad.

But Yumi surprised me by pointing to a sign and saying, "Underground City! Is this what you were referring to in that one email you sent me?"

"Did I send you an email about the Underground City?"

"You mentioned something about going underground...."

I was furious with myself. I didn't recall mentioning it to Yumi, but clearly, I did.

"What do you know about the Underground City?" Mom asked. Now the whole conversation was getting tricky.

"Well, they mention it in Seattle history at school," which was true. I hoped my "lie of omission" would satisfy for the time being.

"I remember hearing something about it," Mom went on, "and thinking, it would be interesting to go on the tour. I guess things are surprisingly preserved from the era. I wouldn't mind checking it out."

I wouldn't mind checking it out, either. If I could get me to keep my mouth shut about "the other" underground city I was quite familiar with.

Both Mom and Yumi were looking at me expectantly, as if I had the deciding vote. Which, I guess I did. "Sure. Okay."

"Don't explode with enthusiasm," Mom said, giving me a yet more intense study.

"I won't."

We trooped to the ticket counter, Mom got three tickets, and we soon found ourselves underground, the loamy, musty scent of earth and ancient wood enveloping us. As it turned out, Mom and Yumi were so engrossed in chatting, and the tour guide so busy telling us fascinating bits of info, that I became entirely caught up in the tour, thinking all the while about the secret underground city that Mitch had discovered, with houses ever so much more intact than on this tour. And, of course, these thoughts became entangled with my thoughts of Millie in the mirror.

I wondered anew about her visitation the night before. What was she trying to tell me? Would I see her again? Would I see the same mysterious, dark room? If I described it to Mitch, would he be familiar with the room?

And *what* was the point of the laser focus on the floorboards?!?

"*Where are you?*" Yumi asked.

"In a galaxy far, far away…." I said, teasing.

"So it seems."

"Is it that obvious?"

"I've never, ever known you to be in a place that was new to you, or see something you've not seen before, and not ask a barrage of questions. When we were just in *Ye Olde Curiosity Shop*, you asked questions about everything—the weird mermaid, the totem poles, even about that strange flavor of gum. And here we are, in a totally, like, *alien* place, and you're as silent as one of those totem poles."

I giggled. The picture of me as a totem pole, with several mouths, whether human, animal or spirit, but all of them silent made a compelling picture. "Nikki as totem pole. Interesting," I said. "Well, I do have something on my mind, and this place has inspired deep thought."

We'd come into another room and listened somberly while the tour guide described the tragic fire that burned down so much of Seattle that day, long, long, ago.

But, again, my mind returned to Mitch's underground city—the intact boardwalk, the beautiful Victorian porches, the intricate wood turning of the spindles and columns. It was a time when attention was paid to minute detail, even out here at land's end, in the wild, wild west. I did have questions. Tons and tons of questions.

Things I saw here reminded me of things in the underground city that Mitch discovered, but there was a sense of a different level of wealth, like a different class, altogether. Mitch's underground city was more affluent. Considerably so, despite the fact that people had to climb a ladder to reach the toilet!

When we came back out of the subterranean city, the sun was heading toward the west.

"Hungry!" I said, my stomach making a little rumble.

"Me too," Mom agreed.

"Me three," Yumi chimed in.

I pointed to a sidewalk cafe across the street with cheerful green and white striped umbrellas over the tables. "How about there?

It has a Victorian look, a perfect stop after our Victorian underground journey. And Dad isn't with us to veto it."

"Good point," Mom nodded. "Let's take advantage of his absence."

We both knew Dad didn't care for restaurants with dainty wrought iron tables and chairs, serving little finger sandwiches and tiny cups of tea. We were soon settled at one such table, our noses in menus that promised tiny sandwiches and diminutive cups of tea.

I felt something rub against my ankle. Looking down, I saw a gray and white striped kitty, making friends with my feet.

"*Lookie!*" I exclaimed, pointing under the table. Mom and Yumi peered under the table.

"Oh, how adorable," Yumi cried.

"Pretty darn cute," Mom agreed. "Completely cinches the atmosphere."

"It does." I reached down and scratched between the kitty's ears, and she began to purr.

Mom ordered cucumber sandwiches and a pot of tea for three, while I puzzled and puzzled over what the cat reminded me of. But I could not bring it to mind.

I heard the buzz of whisper between Mom and Yumi and finally gave them my undivided attention. "What are you two plotting?"

"Not plotting," Yumi said, "Just trying to figure out where you are, and how to get you to come back."

I grinned, feeling guilty. "I'm right here. Just … thinking about all the little pathways the tour took me on. And now this charming restaurant. I feel like I've been dropped into a time about two hundred years ago. Where's my parasol and big hat?"

Right then a motorcycle roared by, and I couldn't hear myself think. I shook my head. "Okay, I'm back." I had to become more present, or they'd start asking me questions that would make me even more uncomfortable. "What was your favorite thing on the tour, Yumi?"

"*Oh!* My favorite thing was the beautiful woodwork," she answered enthusiastically. "The delicate designs of the wood turning, and the scrollwork. Imagine what it must have been like, with the homes full of this art, integrated as part of the home, and probably taken for granted."

I nodded. Yumi and I had taken a woodworking class together our freshman year in high school. "Yeah, I love it, too. I found myself thinking about turning such beautiful spindles. It must have been amazing to be one of those artisans. What about you, Mom? What stood out for you on the tour?"

"My favorite thing was thinking about how real people walked on that boardwalk. Real men and women and children. Busy in their lives … all underground now. All of them, and their city …."

Right at that moment, our waiter brought us our sandwiches and tea.

"And on that uplifting note," I scoffed, "let's enjoy our late lunch!"

Mom tittered. "Sorry! I guess that wasn't a particularly cheerful observation. I did love to see all the Victorian touches, the woodwork you both appreciate, and the faint bits of wallpaper. Imagine when those colors were vibrant."

Yumi and I nodded.

"Fantastic sandwich!" I mumbled around a mouthful.

As we enjoyed our little feast, that kitty continued to keep my ankles company. Why did she choose me?

The waiter came up to us. "Everything to your liking?"

We responded with positive enthusiasm.

"The sandwiches are spectacular," I said. "But I have a question."

"Yes, miss," he said, leaning toward me.

"Why has your cat become so attached to only me?" I gestured under the table.

The waiter and I peered under the table. She looked up at us, purring.

He stood and shrugged. "I've never seen her! Do you want me to attempt to remove her?"

"No. Oh, no. We've formed quite a bond. But ... doesn't she belong to someone here? She seems very much at home."

"No. As I say, I've never seen her."

"She's so cute," Yumi said.

The waiter nodded. "Other than attempted cat removal, which you say you don't need, is there anything else I can do for you?"

"Perhaps more tea," Mom said, pouring the last from the teapot into our cups.

"Of course!" The waiter scurried off with our teapot.

Chapter V
Storm Clouds

After our lazy, delightful, Victorian luncheon, we trekked back to the car and headed for home. I was silently in a "need to see Mitch" frame of mind. I hoped Yumi would be happy to meet him. But the several times I'd mentioned him in our texts and chats, her response had been notably silent. I hadn't thought too much about it. After all, what could she say about someone she'd never met? But now I realized there must be something more going on that I hadn't picked up on.

I decided to wait until we were alone to casually mention that I thought I'd invite him over this evening to meet her. And then I struck upon the brilliant idea to invite Alex as well, and Yumi would not—hopefully!—feel like a third wheel.

I realized it would, in fact, be difficult to give both Yumi and Mitch the undivided attention they were used to getting from me, and it might not be entirely comfortable for all of us. But I was determined to push through. After all, did I intend not to see Mitch the entire time Yumi was here? *No way!*

"Want to hang out with me in my room?" I asked when we got back to the apartment.

"Sure!"

We made a beeline for my room, while Mom, somewhat predictably, found her favorite spot— the piano bench, and began playing something contemporary and light-hearted.

"I love your room," Yumi said, going to one of the long windows and looking down. "It's like being an eagle, up here in the clouds, looking down on the trees."

I joined her. "It is. Sometimes I pretend I'm one of the gargoyles, watching the hurry-scurry of humans below, all tearing around, busy with their business. And I think, "What's so important? Slow down! Take a few moments to take a breath! Sometimes I wonder what everyone is doing. Where is everyone going?"

Yumi nodded thoughtfully. "Yes." One needs to stop and just *be*, sometimes." She glanced up at me, smiling. "That's a very Zen thought you had."

"Hmmmm, nice."

"If they're fortunate," Yumi mused, "they're spending the day doing things they love, being with people they love. If they're very, very fortunate, they'll spend the afternoon going through the Underground City, and then have cucumber sandwiches and tea in the afternoon."

"Of course!" I agreed. "That's exactly what the wisest among them do!" I sat on the edge of the bed and got out my phone. "Sooo ... I was thinking it would be lovely to have you meet Mitch this evening. And then I thought it would be even more lovely if I invited Alex too. I'm sure you'll love them both, like I do. Well," I chuckled, "I wouldn't want you to love Mitch *exactly* like I do!" I expected her to giggle and come back with some quip.

But she didn't. She didn't even turn to look at me, but continued to look down through the clouds to the street below.

"What's up? What are you thinking?" I asked, becoming uncomfortable. I couldn't read her.

"I … I thought, you know, that … I mean, I don't really … okay, I'm a horrible human being, but I don't want to meet Mitch. I don't want to be a third wheel. I thought it would be just you and me. Like today, was so perfect. Of course, your mom is wonderful. I love hanging out with her. But … a boyfriend. I'll be so uncomfortable."

"That's why I'm inviting Alex, too. We'll just be a group of friends. And Mitch and Alex are super wonderful. You're gonna love them!" I tried to be calm and upbeat, but I felt frustrated. I mean, did she honestly think I'd not see Mitch for six weeks? Why hadn't she said anything about this before?

"This thing with Alex, is it a set-up?" She finally turned and looked accusingly at me.

"A set-up? What are you saying? Of course not. Goodness. You know me better than that. Goodness!" Now I was beginning to feel an edge of anger. "Yumi, you needed to have said something before now. Mitch lives next door. Of course I'm

going to hang out with him. I'm mystified that
you'd think I wouldn't."

"I just …." And Yumi burst into tears.

I jumped up, closed the door, and led her to the
bed. I made her sit, and I sat on the floor in front of
her.

"I just … *hate men!*" she exclaimed through her
tears, her body quivering.

"What? … What's going on?" I had no clue
where all this negative passion toward the opposite
gender suddenly came from.

Yumi shook her head, refusing to say more.

"You must tell me!" I insisted.

"Gary …." she whispered.

"Gary? Gary?! Horrible Gary?"

She nodded.

"What about him?"

"After you left, he … he started being so friendly
with me."

"Really! You never mentioned that."

"Well, I know how much you … you know, how
much you dislike him."

"For good reason!"

"Yes. Well. Yes. That's right. You were right. You
were completely right."

"What are you babbling?" I had to pause to
replay the horribleness of Gary—who had pursued
me relentlessly, and then when I tentatively
responded, and we began dating, and I believed
we were 'a couple,' unbeknownst to me, he started
hitting on Marsha, Yumi's and my other best friend.

"Marsha tried to tell me about his advances, but I, in my naiveté, refused to believe it. It's not a thing I could ever do, so I believed the same of him. Until Marsha showed me a couple of his texts. That was the end of Gary. And the end of an entire ocean of innocence and trust in me, too," Yumi blurted out.

"But, Yumi, *why* did you have anything to do with him? You know he's an immoral creep!"

"I don't know. I'm stupid. He wore me down. I believed him."

"Oh, Yumi!" I got up and sat on the bed beside her, putting my arm around her. "Well, now we're both in '*The League of Women Who Know Better than to Go Out with Guys Like Gary.*' Or some such." I succeeded in making her eke out a small giggle.

"I thought you'd be mad at me, or maybe even jealous. Or … or … I don't know. I'm just stupid."

"You're not stupid. And no, I couldn't be mad at you over this. Sad? Yes. Very sad. Remember, I've experienced Gary's so-called charm. His entirely fake, manipulative, charm. So, I understand. But jealous? No way! My goodness, Mitch is a thousand times more interesting, more intelligent, more kind, more loving, and … ahm," I cleared my throat, "more B-E-A-U-T-I-F-U-L than Gary.

"And the same goes for Alex. He is my 'Yumi' here. I mean, he's my best pal. I can tell him anything. He's wise beyond his years. And, bonus, his mom makes the best cherry cheesecake you've ever tasted in your life."

"Yes. I'm looking forward to the cherry cheese-cake," Yumi nodded, hiccupping.

For some reason, that made us both giggle.

"Better now?" I asked, retrieving the box of tissues from my dresser.

"Yes."

"Is it all right if I invite Mitch and Alex over?"

Yumi continued to look down at the tissue in her hands. "Well … yes," she said, very, very, hesitantly.

"The best thing is to face one's fears, not run away from them."

"I know. It's just, it's a lot I've had to process in only a few days. The whole Gary thing blew up last week, and I was so relieved to be coming here and work at putting the disaster behind me. And being here is lovely, but, still, it's a lot of *new*. Everything is new. Seattle, this apartment. And even you. You're the same Nikki. And yet, you're so very different."

"Oh!" I said, stunned. "How am I different?"

"I don't know how to explain it, exactly. You're just … so grown up. You're still Nikki, but you're not a little kid anymore."

"Neither are you! But you're still my Yumi!"

"Yes. I'm still your Yumi. I suppose I must gather my courage and agree to meet these friends of yours—from the enemy camp."

I chuckled. "Be prepared to have a major mind-shift!"

Chapter VI
Friends Together

I texted Mitch and Alex, mentioning to Mitch that Yumi was dealing with an issue that might not let her be her whole wonderful self, and telling Alex a bit more—that she'd recently had her heart broken and needed the "delicate Japanese teacup" treatment.

They both texted in moments with kindness and enthusiasm, Alex affirming that he would come with healing cherry cheesecake.

"All set," I said, returning my attention to Yumi. "They'll be here at seven-thirty, Alex with cheesecake. You will not be able to resist."

"I don't want to resist cheesecake. We'll have to wait and see about the rest."

"All righty!" I jumped up. "Let's tell Mom about the invasion!"

We went into the living room, and I hovered like I do when I want to talk with Mom while she's playing.

She finally paused. "Yes?"

"Mitch and Alex are coming at seven-thirty."

"Lovely!" She turned to Yumi. "You're in for a treat. Two more delightful young men I believe I've never met."

"There! See?" I said as if there was no more argument to be had.

Mom gave me a puzzled look.

"Yumi is hating men at the moment. But I'm determined to change her mind."

"You won't have to. Mitch and Alex will do it in a moment." Mom stood and stretched. "Well, now, I think I'll order a couple of pizzas, how does that sound?"

"Perfect! Thanks, Mom."

At seven-thirty, on the button, the doorbell rang. Just as I opened the door to Mitch—heavenly sight!—the elevator chimed, and down the hall came Alex, with an entire cheesecake (*oh, boy!*) *and* the pizza delivery guy. All of the young men and food crowded into the foyer at once, with chatter and delicious aroma abounding.

Mom hurried to join us, money in hand, and soon the pizzas were in Mitch's hands, the pizza delivery guy gone, and there we stood, looking at one another.

"Confusion!" I exclaimed, giggling. "Yumi probably has no idea who's who, including the pizza delivery guy!" She did, indeed, look bemused.

"The young man holding the pizzas is Mitch, and the one holding cheesecake is Alex. Alex,

Mitch, you finally get to meet my oft-mentioned best childhood friend, Yumi."

They both extended their hands, and in the crowded foyer, food boxes clashed.

"Let's retire to the living room before we end up with food on the floor," Mom suggested.

We found comfy spots on the facing sofas and opened the pizza boxes, while Mom went into the kitchen to gather plates, silverware, and beverages.

"I'll help you," Mitch said, jumping up and following Mom into the kitchen.

Yumi sat on my right side, rather than across from me by Alex, and though a bit crowded, I had to indulge her.

Then I looked at Alex. He had an expression such as I had never seen on his face, and it was directed at Yumi. *Smitten!* Right down to his toes. I caught his glance and, lowering my eyebrows, shook my head a micrometer. Don't go there, I thought. The last thing Yumi needed right now was being pursued by one of my friends! Oh, had I done a wrong thing to invite him? I certainly hadn't expected to see this reaction to her, on sight.

Yes, she's beautiful, with her delicate, translucent Japanese beauty, and her reticent shyness would, of course, be attractive to Alex. But the thought had not crossed my mind that he might fall for her—conspicuously fall for her!—on sight.

And what was worse at this moment was that Yumi may think I'd lied to her, that I did indeed intend to "set her up" with him. But, no. Somewhat strangely perhaps, the thought had never crossed my mind.

"So, Alex, why don't you join the kitchen crew and put the cheesecake on a platter. While we two princesses sit here, waiting to be … waited on?"

"Oh, yes!" Alex jumped up. "Of course. What am I thinking?"

"Good question," I responded, with nuance attached.

Mitch and Mom returned with plates, silverware, and glasses.

Mom paused. "Oh, but wait, would you rather be in the dining room?"

"No, Mom, this is perfect. Close and casual."

Mom nodded, set down the rest of the silverware and napkins. "Okay, I'll let you kids sort it out." She grabbed a slice of pizza and plopped it on a paper plate. "I've got packing to do, so I'll see you later." She disappeared down the hall to her room.

"Packing?" Alex asked, returning with the cheesecake, which, somehow, he found a place for in the midst of our feast on the coffee table.

"Oh, goodness, Alex, I haven't talked to you in several days. Things can change in the Francis family from minute to minute. Mom got a summer job at her school in O.C. teaching at-risk kids in a new summer program. She couldn't be happier.

"For a while there, it looked like they were going to insist I go with them …." I got audible gasps from all three of my friends. "But I made my case, citing that Yumi and I have plenty of 'supervision' with Homer, and Mitch's mom, and Alex's dad. I made a solemn promise to FaceTime with them every day, and to call them the moment anything goes wrong—which it won't!

"We're on 'trial' for a week. If it looks like we can't handle life without them, we'll both have to go to O.C."

"Oh!" Yumi exclaimed. "But my ticket …."

"I know. I told them they'd have to pay for your ticket, because the one you have is nonrefundable, which they understand. Anyway, it's moot, right? We're not going to have any problems, and we're going to have the best time of our lives! Yes?"

"Yes!" Everyone chorused, as we clinked our glasses.

After that bit of bonding, I was happy to see Alex tone down his gawking, and treat Yumi "just like another person" as we chatted about the various things we could do to amuse ourselves. Mitch, Alex, and I were rampant with ideas. Finally, Yumi joined in.

"I wouldn't mind going on the Underground City tour again," she said.

I felt Mitch shift at my side. I gave him a sideways glance. "We went on the Underground City tour today. I believe Yumi enjoyed it quite a lot."

"I did. That would be why I said I'd like to go again." She poked me in the ribs, teasing.

"*Yeah!* We could do that," Alex agreed.

"And then go to the little restaurant across the street. I wonder if that cat will be there again?" I added.

"Cat?" Mitch asked.

"So strange! There was a little gray cat under the wrought iron table, purring and rubbing my ankles. I asked the waiter if she was the restaurant's mascot, but he said he'd never seen her."

"She was *so cute*," Yumi added. "Gray and white striped, but only interested in Nikki."

"True. And yet, when we got up to leave, she'd completely disappeared. I was sort of glad because the street had so much traffic, and I was worried that she might try to follow me. But … she was gone!"

"Curious," Mitch said thoughtfully.

"Yes. Curious." I moved to sit by Alex. The way we were lined up in front of him was too much like a game show, with Mitch, Yumi, and me the participants and Alex, the game show host. Yumi would take it the wrong way—for sure!—if I asked her to sit by him. Mitch wrinkled his brow a bit, but shrugged.

While we babbled on about the different things we *must do* to entertain ourselves in the ensuing weeks, I became more and more disconcerted to see how beautiful Yumi and Mitch looked together. They weren't together, of course. They were at opposite ends of the sofa. But there was no getting around how gorgeous they were, nearly side-by-side. I became more preoccupied with *how to shut my brain up* from these thoughts than the discussion at hand.

"Nikki?" Alex's voice intruded on my thoughts, "Where'd you go?"

"Oh," I chuckled. "Off with the fairies, I guess. What did I miss?"

"I asked when your parents were coming back."

"I don't know, exactly. A couple of months, I guess. But I imagine one or the other of them will come up sometime during the summer to do a spot check. Make sure the apartment building is still here, little stuff like that."

"We'll have to make sure that it is," Alex said.

"Yes. Let's. For one thing, it's nice to have a place to live, but what's even more important, I don't want to be grounded for my entire junior year of high school!"

"Good plan," Mitch agreed. "And it's going to be such a great year! My first full year of going to public school. And with you, Nikki, and Alex there in the halls, and having lunch together—I'm so looking forward to it."

"Your first year of school!" I exclaimed. "Kindergarten!"

We laughed, and Mitch nodded. "In some ways, it will be. One of the most important aspects of kindergarten is socialization. With my sheltered life of home-schooling, no peers in my world until Nikki, I can use some socialization."

"You can teach us a bit about socialization!" I protested. "You're kind, polite, mature. You're a fantastic listener…."

"Absolutely!" Alex agreed. "You're a true friend, thoughtful, generous …."

Mitch squirmed a bit. "Stop, please. I wasn't fishing!"

"You don't need to." Oh, I so wanted to just jump up and give him a big kiss. But I restrained myself … for the moment. "You're all those things, and more, and that's from your two best friends, who really know who you are." I glanced at Alex. "Maybe we need to give him a negative review, so he'll have something to work on in his kindergarten-socialization class."

"You're probably right …."

But silence fell as we tried to come up with something Mitch could work on. After a few moments of blank silence, we burst into giggles.

"I guess you're perfect!" Alex declared.

"Agreed," I said. "Okay, I'm ready for cheese-cake. Who's with me?"

A chorus rang out from everyone, so I proceeded to cut huge wedges of cheesecake and plop them on plates. I handed the first one to Yumi.

"That's too much," she protested.

"Take it! You'll change your mind!"

"All right," she hesitantly agreed.

The three of us watched intently as she had her first bite.

"*Oh! My! Goodness!*" she exclaimed. "This is heavenly! I've never tasted anything like it! Your mother makes this?"

"She does," Alex affirmed.

"She's truly talented."

Alex grinned. "Thanks, I'll tell her you said so."

Yumi continued to devour the cheesecake as if she feared it would get up and run away.

"There's plenty more," I said, handing giant wedges to Mitch and Alex. Thinking about Alex's talented mother brought Yumi's mom to mind. "Yumi's mother is also incredibly talented. She creates a line of clothes I just love. It always has a subtle hint of the Orient—it's almost mystical. Mom buys something from her line every year."

"Oh, Nikki!" Yumi said, surprised.

"What?"

"I didn't know you even noticed my mom's work, let alone that you have such a high opinion of it."

"I've told you *lots* of times that I love your mom's creations."

"I thought you were being polite!"

"No, I truly love her work. One day I'll be adult enough—and hopefully rich enough!—to occasionally buy the perfect piece from *Mika Miyake Fashions*."

"Okay, we're just a couple of guys, but I hope, Yumi, you'll let us see some of your mom's work," Alex said.

"Yes," Mitch piped up. "I know next to nothing about fashion beyond a clean shirt and jeans. But I enjoy art, and, from what Nikki's saying, your mom produces art."

"She does," Yumi said shyly. "Right now she's doing preliminary sketches for next spring. But the fall line is so … so … I told her she's completely outdone herself. There's a lot of envy in the industry. The spring line is going to break a lot of designers' hearts—she'll have creations they've never come close to thinking of." She looked shyly down at her nearly empty plate, a pale blush making her, if possible, even more beautiful, on the heels of her monologue.

"I can't wait to see it," I said. "Maybe Mom and I will come down for her show."

"That would be wonderful, Nikki." She finished her cheesecake. "I can't believe I ate it all! But I'm suddenly very tired, do you mind if go to bed?"

"Of course not!" I said. "It was a jam-packed day, and another one tomorrow. Sleep sweet—I'll see you in the morning."

Yumi stood, and Mitch and Alex leapt to their feet. Such gentlemen!

"In the morning …." She said softly, waving and making her way down the hall to the conservatory. Mitch and Alex turned to give me a questioning look.

After I heard the glass door click shut I softly told them, "She fell in love with the conservatory on sight. She and Mom wheeled the rollaway in there last night. I think it's a great idea, and kind of wonder why I've never thought of sleeping in there on occasion myself."

"*Brilliant!*" Alex exclaimed. "It's an amazing space. Very clever of her to lay claim to it." He paused. "She … she's also sort of amazing."

"Yes, she is. But, Alex, please, don't make any advances."

"Make advances? I've never 'made advances' to any girl in my life. I'm pretty sure I don't know how to. And I won't do anything, or at least I wouldn't intend to do anything that she could take as 'an advance.' Is it okay if I'm just friendly?"

I couldn't tell if he was sincere or sarcastic, although sarcastic would be unlike him.

"Of course, Mr. Goofy. Be friendly. Like you were tonight, most of the time. Except for those bits of googly eyes."

Alex acted offended. "Good grief! I'm a dog with bulging eyes. I wonder that you even invited me over."

"I have but one word. 'Cheesecake.'"

"Oh, yes. Of course." He bowed. "You've made the terms of my admission to the castle clear. I shall do my best to avert my goofy, googly eyes when in the presence of the esteemed princesses."

I punched him in the biceps. "Evermore goofy!"

Mitch chuckled. "I think the poor servant has been abused enough."

Alex looked from me to Mitch, and back to me. "Ah! Third wheel. I'm outta here." He stood. "Anyway, I've got to get up early and do some deliveries for Dad. I guess I'll see you tomorrow after that. We did all that chatter about the things we're going to do, without resolving what we'd do tomorrow!"

"True," I agreed. "But I think we're happy just hanging out together, aren't we?"

"Yes," Alex and Mitch chorused enthusiastically.

Alex gathered his paper plates, silverware, and cup. "Want me to wrap up the cheesecake and put it in the fridge?"

"Sure!" I felt too lazy to clear the coffee table at that moment, plus I feared Mitch might take it as his cue to leave. And I didn't want him to leave.

I moved to sit by Mitch. He put his arm around me as we listened to Alex's kitchen-fussing. He soon came out and headed for the door. We watched him, comfortably ensconced.

"No, no. Don't get up," he quipped.

"All righty," I answered. "See you tomorrow."

"Alone at last!" I sighed as the door clicked shut, snuggling cozily into Mitch's side. After all, I'd not seen him since before Dad left, and that was two whole days. "What do you think of Yumi?"

"She's very sweet. I can see why you're best friends."

"How so?"

"You complement each other. And you clearly care deeply for one another. But—tell me more about what's going on with her that you hinted at in your text."

"Do you remember my mentioning a boy that I said you were the opposite of in every imaginable way?"

"Yes. Gary."

I was impressed! "What a memory."

"About someone you were emotionally involved with? Sure, I remember every detail."

"Well, the short story is, he did the same thing to Yumi that he did to me. And, right now, she's hating men. All men. Although I hope tonight turns her around about a couple of very special men, who are not one bit like that."

"But … I'm confused, you're saying she got involved with the very same person that treated you horribly?"

"Yes."

"And she knew everything that had happened between you and this Gary person?"

"Yes. Oh, yes. She knew about it, in moment-by-moment playoffs."

"But … why would she … I mean … I don't understand."

"I said pretty much the same thing to her. But then I remembered the immensity of his charm. Unreal, but powerful for naive young women like Yumi and me. I told her the quote I read recently. 'I fell in love with the person you pretended to be.' That's Gary."

"Meanwhile, our friend has fallen for her, hook, line, and sinker, like a ton of bricks," Mitch said almost under his breath.

"Dusting off the mixed metaphor clichés … you're right, he fell, as you say, like a ton of bricks. Or through a black hole."

"Always plenty of thrills in Nikki's home!"

"Hmmm," I replied, haunted by my mirror. The appearance of Millie and the underground city having gone around and around in the back of my mind all day. I wanted to mention it to Mitch, but something held me back. I could tell him anytime. But I couldn't *un-tell* him if I shared it now.

"By the way, thanks for not mentioning my underground city to Yumi and your mom," he said as if reading my mind. "That must have been a challenge, given how much more amazing my section of it is than what's on the tour."

"It *was* a bit of a challenge. But it's your secret, and not mine to tell."

"I'm thinking, though, that it would probably be all right to share my underground city with our two closest friends. They aren't going to tell anyone, and since Yumi was so captivated by the tour, I'm sure she'd enjoy my 'tour.' What do you think?"

Why did I hesitate? I felt a foreboding that I couldn't express. "We could … I suppose."

"Why the hesitation?"

"I don't know … something. Maybe it's not safe. Maybe … I don't know. You're right, Yumi would love it."

He took in my hesitation without pushing. One of the many reasons I love him. "I guess we need to contemplate it a bit more," he said. "Anyway, there's plenty of activities to keep us occupied."

"Yes, there's plenty to do." Then a thought hit me like a lightning bolt. "*But, wait!* Oh, I'm a big old clod. What's the matter with me? You have news. *You have news!* What's your news, and why didn't you share it with us this evening?"

"I wanted to tell just you, first. Plus I didn't want to take the attention off Yumi, as my news has nothing to do with her."

"Okay. All right. Fine. Stop stalling, *tell me!*"

"It might not be a big deal. But it is to me."

"Yes-yes-yes. Goodness! *Speak!*"

"I got a summer internship with an attorney."

I was shocked. "Did I know you were looking for a summer internship with an attorney?"

Mitch registered his own shock. "Not the response I was anticipating."

I paused for a moment. This was a Big Deal. He needed my kudos and support. He'd told me he wanted to become an attorney. That his heritage of a family who prided themselves on ripping people off was the single most important thing he wanted to change. He was a home-schooled seventeen-year-old, and he had *managed to get a summer internship with an attorney!*

But ... selfish, tiny, little Nikki whined, what about our summer?! I needed to have a very serious talk with this nasty Nikki. "I'm a terrible person, Mitch. Of course, it's fantastic and amazing. But please don't be upset if I ask why didn't I know you were planning on getting a summer internship?"

"I guess I didn't think it through. I couldn't imagine I'd actually get an internship. And, it seemed better, if I—somehow!—succeeded in getting one, to have it be a surprise."

"*It's a surprise.* When do you start? What will you be doing? Where is it?"

"I'll start in two weeks, so we have time to do a bunch of the things we talked about tonight. I suppose I'll mostly be a gofer. But it'll be great, because I'll see what it's like to be an attorney. I'll learn so much! The office is near here—Watson & Watson. They mostly do family law, protecting the innocent. I'm pretty darn pleased."

I couldn't help falling in love with him more, if it was possible. His enthusiasm was contagious! "When did you find out?"

"Friday, while you were taking your dad to the airport and getting Yumi. I've been bursting with it. I told my mother, of course. But I just wanted to tell you, Nikki."

"Again, I'm a terrible person, and I apologize, some more, for my initial response. Or lack of. I was in shock. I think you can take that as the response you wanted, because it's so big! If I'd just said, 'oh, that's nice,' that would have been a disappointing response."

Mitch chuckled, hugging me closer. "You're right. And adorable."

We reveled in Mitch's triumph quietly. Oh, yes, it felt so delicious, being held by the *Love of my Life*, and sharing his success.

But, irritation!—that old, nasty, "I am not worthy" litany raised its ugly voice, making me wonder what he found in me that made me equal to his sure sense of self, his sense of purpose, and his whole adult perspective.

"You're so amazing," I whispered.

He leaned down and we shared a long, sweet kiss. "So are you," he whispered back. "Everything makes sense in my life, knowing you care about me."

"I care about you, I love you. But I'm just a *kid*, and you're this grown-up person."

"I'm not grown-up and you're not a kid," he dared to argue.

"Okay," I answered, simply. For the moment, I liked that response very much.

"So!" He stirred about. "As much as I could stay right here, just like this, all night, tonight, and tomorrow, and the next day, and the next, I think I'd better go home. You have a guest, your Mom's leaving day after tomorrow, and we've got plans for a big day, so off I go, wishing you the sweetest of dreams." He kissed my forehead and stood.

I knew he was right. But, oh! I didn't want him to leave. "See? You prove my point. Adult behavior!" I stood, and we walked to the door, where we shared another lingering kiss before he ambled down the hall to his apartment. I stood in my doorway enjoying the beauty of his movement until he disappeared behind his own door.

In a mist of happiness and confusion—I made my way to my room.

Chapter VII
The Mystical Cat

Wide awake and *full* of mixed thoughts and happy feelings, I contemplated getting out Grammy's emerald ring and having a good long talk with her. But first, I thought, I ought to decide what I'd wear tomorrow. I was leaning toward going to the Museum of Pop Culture, and then if we had time, checking out Archie McPhee's. Good for a few laughs, and, weirdly, I almost always bought some strange trinket.

But—and why didn't I know this would happen the minute I stepped into my closet?—up through the swirling sepia of the mirror floated Millie the Milliner. Something serious was brewing. I didn't like how it felt. *But I could not turn away.*

I expected the image to fade to the boardwalk and to be taken into the bowels of the underground city. But, no. The image remained fixed on Millie. As I watched, her features changed, shifted, ever so slightly, becoming more delicate, her skin glowing and almost translucent. As her features changed, so did the letters in her name. After a stunning transformation, I found myself staring at a young woman who looked unnervingly like Yumi, and the letters of Millie's name had shifted to Meechie.

Movement in the lower right corner of the mirror took my attention, and *there!* … there was that little gray and white striped cat, hurrying on the boardwalk into the depths of darkness. She paused and looked over her shoulder at me, like, *"come along now!"*

I stood before the mirror, calmly watching the little cat. No. Not calmly. *Stunned,* I watched the little cat. She scurried into the darkness. I could just barely see her as she ran up the stairs of the porch the mirror had shown me before. The front door stood slightly ajar, and the cat ran inside the house.

Now I heard voices! And not just any voices, but the voices of my three best friends. I heard Yumi exclaim over something, but I couldn't make out her words.

Then came a loud scraping, squeaking, squawking sound. I followed the cat through the house, and my friends' voices became louder. The squawking sound turned into a sort of crunching sound, like metal in a contest with wood.

Then Alex said, "We've got it!"

I entered the room I'd seen before, and watched as the forms of my friends—bending over something—faded and disappeared….

Oh! This must be a warning not to go to Mitch's underground city!

I looked around for the little cat, but I didn't see her, either. As the image faded, I faced myself in the mirror, terror on my features. My mind raced as I left the closet, disoriented, shocked, alarmed. In simplest terms, *freaking out.*

Did Millie—or Meechie—disapprove of me and my three friends in "her" underground city?

I was tempted to put a sheet over the mirror again, like I'd done before. But I knew I wouldn't because now it showed my friends *disappearing.*

Alarming. *ALARMING!*

*   *

Somehow I managed to fall asleep. I woke up very early in the morning with the sun making a quiet appearance, stirring about my room. I was happy to see that it looked like it would be another sunny day. After the events of the night before, I was not in the mood for darkness.

I replayed the whole scene the mirror showed me, and realized, as it came to the end after my friends disappeared, the view had stayed steady for quite some time. I was so shocked to see my friends fade and disappear, I didn't even notice that the scene remained for as much as a minute before fading altogether. And I realized that I'd missed a great opportunity to look around and take in details *… I should have explored the room in the vision.*

I sat on the edge of my bed, head in hands, frustrated—how could I have missed what was probably the whole point of the vision? I shook my head in irritation.

Yumi knocked at my door. "You awake?"

I pulled myself together, sitting up, crossed-legged on the bed. "Yeah. Come in."

She gave me a strange look as she came to stand by me. "Are you wearing the same thing you wore yesterday?"

I had fallen asleep without even bothering to get into my pjs.

"Ah, no. I guess I fell asleep in my clothes." I needed to stop doing that!

"Strange!"

No argument there. I was behaving strangely—and things around me were behaving strangely. "Yeah. Strange."

Yumi sat cross-legged on the bed facing me. "So … what are we doing today?"

I wanted to say, "We're not going anywhere near any part of the underground city." But I said, instead, "I think you'll enjoy the Museum of Pop Culture, more affectionately known as MoPop."

"Oh, yes," Yumi nodded enthusiastically. "I'd like that. I watched a few YouTubes about it after you mentioned it. It looks fantastic!"

I nodded. "We can take the monorail, which is a fun, too." I glanced out the window. "It looks like it's going to be another sunny day. I'm glad you packed a lot of sunshine in your backpack. I've come to love the drizzly rain, but if we're running around from place to place, sunshine is nice." I threw my legs over the edge of the bed, ready to jump up, setting the phantasmagorical world I'd been contemplating aside, and getting into the real world of the here and now. "I'd better get in motion!"

"Yes …." Yumi said, with a pause.

"Yes?"

"I want … I need to … talk about … Alex."

"Okay." I sat back on the bed.

But she remained silent. "Yumi, dear, you must make some sounds if you need to talk."

She giggled. "That seems to be the hard part. Well, I just … please make him stop looking at me like he did last night," she blurted. "I just don't want … you know. I told you already."

"O-k-a-a-a-y." I felt irritated. Yes, he'd been taken by her beauty—who wouldn't be?—but he'd been the perfect picture of polite. It was not my job to police him if he found her attractive. I shook my head.

"Actually, Yumi, *not* okay. Alex is a very sweet guy. And he's also very much what-you-see-is-what-you-get. He's transparently honest. You're beautiful. He saw your beauty. He appreciated it. He also liked you as a person. So no, I will not even attempt to try to 'make him stop looking at you.' I was there. He did nothing wrong or inappropriate."

I reached out and took her delicate little hands in mine. "I think this is a great opportunity for you to release some fears. You're safe with us, with me and Mitch and Alex. If Alex does anything out of line—and he won't—I'll say something to him. But otherwise, my dearest friend, you'll have to be just a bit less of a princess, and a tad more grown up."

Wow! Where did that come from? I had no idea I could be so straightforward.

Yumi tried to pull her hands from me, but I wouldn't let go. And I refused to look away from my direct eye contact. She looked down, and relaxed. "Who are you?" she asked softly.

"I'm me, your own Nikki. Your friend who loves you—who has a first-hand idea of the pain you're processing. I'm your friend who knows you'll soon forget all about Gary, a small, passing experience in a life full and rich with real love and real friends."

She looked up at me endearingly, as only Yumi could. "You're right. *You are right.* In every way, with everything you say. I apologize for … for being a princess. Yes. Spoiled! What was I thinking, telling you to make someone else behave in a certain way? Kinda nuts, huh? I'll do my best to set my fears aside." She pulled her hands from mine and leaned forward and gave me a hug.

"That took a lot of bravery, Nikki, to talk to me like that. But it was the most amazing thing you could have done for me. You're the best friend ever!"

"Oh!" With a quavery voice I added, "And my two 'opposite gender' friends are like me, as well."

"Yes," Yumi said. "I will keep that in mind and stop being judgmental." She scooted off the bed. "Now then, get yourself presentable, and I'll do the same. I'm ravenous. Meet you in the kitchen for breakfast?"

"I'll be there!"

Chapter VIII
The Emerald City

We had to wait for Alex to finish his dad's deliveries, but the four of us were on the monorail by eleven-thirty, which was good enough. Yumi *ohh-ed* and *ahh-ed* at the city as the monorail zipped along, and Mitch, Alex, and I sat back proudly, as if we'd built the beautiful city ourselves.

The Gorgeous Emerald City I had come to love.

I'd only been to MoPop once, and that, of course, with my parents. So this was an entirely new experience for me, too. Mom had treated us with buying the tickets online, so we waltzed in like we owned the place.

I braced for overwhelm!

The museum used to be called the Music Experience, or something like that, so there's a lot about the amazing rise of contemporary music, and more guitars than you'd think were on the planet. Guitars owned by really famous musicians who changed the world with their poetry and music— music that anyone could carry around in their mind and hum. Pop music had, for sure, *changed the world*.

"Video games!" Alex called, as he rushed forward into the video game section.

There were rows and rows of video games, old and new. After awhile of mostly watching Alex and Mitch apparently determined to play every one of them, I called a halt.

"Come on, guys, we want to see everything!"

"Agreed," Yumi said softly.

Somewhat reluctantly Alex and Mitch joined Yumi and me as we came to the tribute to horror films.

Which, okay, I don't really understand horror movies. I have enough scary stuff I'm dealing with, without the images of monsters getting stuck in my mind. I wasn't much fun there, either, as I mostly stood around without going through the whole scary place. Again, the guys really got into it.

What can I say? They were getting my mom's money's worth.

Then, *finally!* we came to the science fiction section— my favorite section after the music memorabilia. I loved strolling down memory lane with the **Star Trek** displays. But, again, the alien monsters I skirted, not needing to see them 'live and in the flesh.'

I somehow ended up on my own. Alex and Mitch became engaged in a deep intellectual discussion about the animatronics of a particular monster. They were brain-deep in sorting out what parts of the movie—I have no idea which movie— were CG, and which parts had been enacted by the animatronic creature before them, to which they appeared to be paying obeisance.

I'd lost track of Yumi, and as I wandered about looking for her, I finally I came upon her, transfixed, in front of the display of Dorothy's dress from *The Wizard of Oz*. She appeared so deeply entranced, that I didn't want to bother her. Something had struck a chord with her, and I left her to her musing.

I, of course, have always adored the Tin Man, without a heart, but so kind and full of heart. I stood before him thinking about how life is all a lesson about heart and love.

Finally, we found ourselves together again, and we staggered out of the museum, exhausted from so much fun.

Even though exhausted and staggering, I grinned from ear to ear. "Did we have fun, or what?"

"We had fun!" Mitch and Alex chorused.

I glanced at Yumi who remained noticeably quiet. "Are you okay?"

She started, as if coming out of a trance. "I'm … fantastic. Just … so much to process. Lots to think about. All that so-called 'pop culture' shaping the world we live in. Much of the science fiction were the dreams of writers in days past, and now, so many of those fantastic imaginings have become realities. Hoverboards and cell phones and … just so many creative thoughts from the past are our reality …."

We stood in a knot around her, listening raptly.

"Brilliant!" Alex exclaimed. "The world we live in was imagined by creators over the past decades, with their creativity becoming our realities, to our advantage!"

"Yes," I said, unable to keep from teasing, "just as long as the monsters don't also become real!"

"Let's hope not!" Mitch laughed and put his arm around me. "I'll protect you!"

I chuckled, as I leaned into him, feeling delightfully safe and warm.

We then jumped on the monorail to return home, the day too far spent to go to Archie McPhee's. Yumi sat by me, and as the monorail was crowded, Mitch and Alex had to find seats a few rows away.

"What was your single most favorite thing?" I asked, pretty sure what she would answer, but curious to know more about why.

"My single most favorite thing … and I know this is probably going to sound a bit unbelievable with all the amazing things at MoPop … but my favorite thing was Dorothy's little pinafore and blouse. Awed, I stood there thinking, "This is the real dress that Judy Garland wore in *The Wizard of Oz*. It completely took my imagination."

I nodded, sharing her sense of awe.

"Because … because my mom and I watch *The Wizard of Oz* every year. But more than that, she told me, years ago, when I was just a little, little girl, maybe five years old, she told me that she got into clothing design because of that little outfit that Dorothy wore. She said it so charmed her when she was a little girl, it made her want to create clothes that were, somehow, charming in their own way.

"And then, as I stood there, I thought about the Emerald City in *The Wizard of Oz*, and that Seattle is the Emerald City. All of those thoughts welled up in me to make me feel like there was something more … a reason bigger than I know … for me to be here. Some kind of ….”

“Fate?”

“Yes. Some kind of fate. Strange, strange feeling. But, there it was. There *it is*. I still feel it. It’s kind of disorienting.”

I nodded like I knew what she was saying. But I was plunged into anxiety, matching up her sense of fate with my three precious friends disappearing in the mirror’s vision.

What did fate have in mind? And could I keep harm from coming to my friends?

*   *

We agreed that we’d had enough adventure for the day and were ready for dinner. I promised to make my famous quick and easy spaghetti. I texted Mom the plan as we got off the monorail and walked to Zingas Grocery, where I needed to get the few odds and ends for dinner. But even more important, to introduce Yumi to Alex’s dad.

The little bell above the door jangled noisily as the four of us crowded into the shop. Mr. Zingas glanced at us with a grin as he helped a customer. Our chatty energy filled the whole store and the customer finished her purchase and scurried through the door as quickly as she could.

"Look at these beautiful young people," Mr. Zingas proclaimed, his grin overtaking his entire face. "This must be the esteemed Miss Yumi, whom I've heard so much about. Ah, my dear, your fame precedes you."

Yumi giggled, looking down. Does she even have a clue how incredibly adorable she is when she does that?

"I'm sure there's nothing of fame about me," she said softly.

"I believe you are incorrect," Mr. Zingas teased. But I could see he understood her discomfort, and he turned his attention to the rest of us.

"So! Did you all have a good time at MoPop?"

We all—even Yumi—started babbling at once, telling him about our spectacular day, each of us desirous of telling our own particular story.

"Wonderful! Wonderful! *Won-der-ful!*" Mr. Zingas proclaimed.

I recalled the reason I was here and excused myself. "I've promised to make dinner, so I must gather some goods." I grabbed a shopping basket and ran around the store gathering French bread, tomatoes, lettuce, angel hair spaghetti—there was probably some in the cupboard, but I wanted to be sure I had enough—and a few other bits, then rejoined my friends, who had all, including Mr. Zingas, seated themselves at one of the little tables.

As I came up, I was surprised to see Yumi, sitting near Mr. Zingas, enthusiastically telling him a shortened version of her experience contemplating Dorothy's outfit. The sight of them all leaning forward, happily together, sharing the moment, made my heart leap with joy.

How beautiful and sweet and precious they were! I took a mental snapshot, knowing I would never, *never*, forget this picture.

"*Ahm* … I hate to interrupt this delightful bonding among you. But if I'm to make dinner, I'd better get at it. You can stay and chat, but I need to pay for my goods." I held up my basket. "And get home."

Everyone stood. "No, we'll come with you," Alex said. "We'll continue the bonding another time."

Mr. Zingas rang up my purchases and we walked to the apartment, still full of chatter. Homer smiled upon us as if we were his own children, as he held the door open.

"Looks like you've had a good day," he said.

"Thank you, Homer," Mitch replied, "We've had a *great* day!"

Yes, a great day, I thought. May they all be like this. We rode the elevator up and trundled down the hall.

When I unlocked the door, there stood three suitcases.

And, well, it kind of knocked me for a loop. Mom was leaving tomorrow. The moment I'd been looking forward to, now hit me hard.

Mom was leaving me tomorrow! Dad was already gone!

I'd never been apart from my parents more than four days at summer camp, years ago. And, at that time, they were only twenty miles away.

Oh. My. Goodness. It hit me. I felt strange, like they were willfully abandoning me. Not at all as if I'd begged and cajoled for this outcome.

Was I grown up enough to live on my own? Well, not entirely on my own, with adults at every turn.

But … no parents.

Mom stopped playing the piano when we came in. She came over to us, all smiles, but took one look at me, and knew exactly what I was feeling.

And … her smile shifted to the same expression I was feeling. "I know, Nikki. Me too. But we must be brave."

My friends stepped back, so sensitive, every one of them! giving us space. Mom put her arms around me, and whispered, "It'll be just fine, Pumpkin Patch."

Now, her calling me one of Dad's pet names for me—which she *never* did—just about undid me. Tears threatened.

"I know," I whispered back. "And … if it doesn't work …."

"You can be on the next plane to O.C."

"Right." I sighed deeply. "Well, I have a promised dinner to make, so …."

"Am I lucky or what," Mom giggled, turning to my friends. "I have a daughter who will make dinner for her friends and me, allowing me to spend the last couple hours getting as much bonding with the baby grand piano as I can squeeze in."

Chapter IX
On Our Own

I thought I'd probably be in the kitchen, slaving away by myself while my friends hung out in the living room. But, to my surprise, they all insisted on crowding into the kitchen to help me. Alex got busy peeling the veggies, Yumi took it upon herself to set the table in the dining room—as we were five people, and it was a "real dinner," with several serving dishes, we needed the actual dining room table. Mitch busied himself as my sous chef, handing me utensils, stirring the sauce, and otherwise adorably being underfoot.

In honor of our day at MoPop, Mom sat at the piano and played pop music. Songs by Paul McCartney, Sting, David Bowie, Prince. Songs that, surprisingly, we knew—I suppose because they've been covered again and again by so many artists. Anyway, it put us in a delightful mood, and my simple little dinner came together beautifully!

Soon we gathered all the dishes to take into the dining room and put on the sideboard. But what a surprise when I walked into the dining room! Yumi had not only set the table, lit candles, and turned the room lighting down low, she'd also brought in several plants from the conservatory and placed them around the room. Against the rich dark wood of the walnut wainscoting, it was gorgeous and warm and cozy.

Mom joined us at the door, and we all said, *"Ohhhh!"* together as if we'd rehearsed it.

"The plants, Yumi!" I exclaimed. "Fantastic! The room looks like it belongs on the cover of *Beautiful Homes*."

"Yes," Mom agreed. "This room, as lovely as it is, is a bit formal for our family's taste. But the plants make it altogether friendly."

Mom hit the nail on the head. I'd been a tiny bit reluctant to have our dinner in the dining room, because, although gorgeous, it seemed a bit unfriendly. *Not so now!*

We bustled about, organizing the serving dishes and finding a place to sit—strangely, the table didn't seem as big as before.

"I hope you don't mind that I took a leaf out of the table," Yumi said as if in response to my thought. "It felt like it would make us too far apart. With the leaf, the table seats ten, but without it, it seats six comfortably."

"Oh, perfect! Why haven't we thought of that, Mom?"

"I don't know! You're so clever, Yumi."

"Oh, no," Yumi demurred. "I just wanted this meal to be as nice as possible before you leave tomorrow. A good memory ...."

"A very good, very sweet, memory," Mom affirmed.

We all mumbled our agreement, and then, without further procrastination, fell to eating. My friends happily engaged in sharing with Mom their experiences of the day at MoPop. I let the sound of their voices ebb and flow around me, while the anxious feelings I needed to process took up my mind. Not only had I still not come to a place where I felt I could release the disturbing vision in the mirror, but now, added to that, was my surprising feelings of … I had to name it … *abandonment. Weird.* But—Mom was leaving.

I couldn't be more surprised with myself. Everything was fine, and everything was *going to be fine.* But I felt, somehow, that was not true.

"Did you still like the music section best?" Mom asked me. "Or did some other area become your new favorite?"

"I still like the music best, and science fiction next. All those guitars, all the incredibly talented people who played them, all the thoughts and feelings that went into that creativity, in such a short while. Pop culture blossomed suddenly on humanity and changed the world. It's kinda interesting, isn't it?"

Mom looked at me like, who are you? "You're right, Nikki. It is strange and interesting how all of those new creations in music and literature and film bloomed in a short time, as you say, and became available for everyone, not just the elite."

This triggered a conversation that flowed around the table during the meal, and I, after setting the topic in motion, went back to my dark musings. Everyone understood that I was sad about Mom leaving, and they left me to my silence, with the occasional glance of kindness and love.

I dreaded to think what they would have to say if they knew that the darkest of my reflections was my fear of them disappearing.

*   *

After we cleared away dinner, we each took a couple of plants back to their spots in the conservatory so they could get their morning sun.

"*Goodness!* Yumi, how did you carry all these plants yourself? Some of them are huge and heavy," I exclaimed, lugging one such from room to room.

"I'm strong!" she quipped, flexing her tiny biceps, making all of us laugh.

After everything was in place, I got out the Monopoly board and set it up on the coffee table in the living room. "Mom, are you going to play with us?"

"Oh … no. You kids have fun."

"Please play with us," Mitch cajoled. "I'm going to miss you, and I'd like to spend some time with you."

Well, he simply manages to continually make me love him more! I knew he was telling the truth, because he truly likes Mom. Sometimes, in fact, I think he likes her more than me. How many times have I come into the room, and they have their heads together, deep in conversation?

Like him, I wanted Mom to play Monopoly with us. She never cares in the least whether she wins or loses, she just enjoys the companionship. Dad and I both have a "gotta win" gene, which, quite frankly, I don't much care for. I'd rather be like Mom. But in the heat of the game, that thought goes away.

What's even more frustrating—*she almost always wins!* Sometimes Dad and I'll be growling because she's just won at a game and she'll ask, innocently, "Whose turn?" We'll inform her that the game is over because she's just won. Then she giggles and says, "Oh! I had no idea!"

I was curious to see how her laissez-faire attitude would come into play with us tonight, as we settled into our places, Mom and Alex on one sofa facing Mitch and Yumi on the other. I preferred to sit at the end of the game board on the floor, so I could get right up close and personal. I intended to put everything I had into the game to take my mind off my other, counter-productive, not-getting-anywhere, circling worrisome thoughts.

I started out gobbling up every property in sight, worse than any slumlord, ever. Everyone, but Mom, of course, was moaning at my incredible luck as I demanded sky-rocketing rents, and showed no mercy.

Ah! This was the way to play the game! Mom landed on one of my many-housed properties.

"You owe me tons of rent!" I chortled.

"Okay," Mom smiled, gesturing at her money. "Take what you need."

"Don't let her do that," Alex protested. "She's an evil slumlord, not to be trusted."

"Oh no," Mom said. "She's my sweet little girl, who would not harm a flea."

"Well, Mrs. F," Mitch added, "We're not fleas, and she's doing us in. Maybe we should flee."

I laughed my most evil, terrible, slumlord laugh. "Nowhere to flee! I'll charge you rent, wherever you go, *more rent. Ha-ha-ha!*"

Everyone chuckled at my drama, but Mom said, "Well, I'd suggest to the evil slumlord that she may discover the faster the ride, the harder the fall."

And with that, as if she'd waved a magic wand, I *fell!* Within fifteen minutes, somehow—*somehow!*—Mom had all my properties. She refused to charge the rent that all those houses I'd accumulated were worth. Even me, the evil slumlord, she only charged the face value of the property.

I should have known! Despite her efforts to be generous, she soon pretty much owned the board, and the game was over.

We all sat back in silence, a bit stunned because what had transpired was practically mystical.

"How did you *do* that?" Alex finally whispered.

"I didn't do anything. Other, of course, than enjoy being with you beautiful young people. Sitting here feeling reassured that you'll be responsible young adults, taking care of one another. Which is all I ask. That you be just as you are, looking out for one another, enjoying one another's company, being kind and loving."

"Well, except for Nikki," Yumi protested. "She was horrible and selfish."

"Perhaps, but you see the outcome? What works, and what will always work, is thinking about the other person's feelings, and making sure you don't add to their woes." Mom stood and stretched. "I'm off to bed. I need to talk with your dad for a bit, Nikki, and I have a big day tomorrow."

"Sleep tight, Mom."

"You too, Sweetie."

"Good night, good night," all my friends called to her, then fell silent as we heard the bedroom door softly close.

Her departure pulled something from the energy we'd generated during the evening, and we agreed it was time to get some sleep. Alex and Mitch put the Monopoly game away, while Yumi went off to the conservatory.

"See you tomorrow?" Alex asked.

"Of course." I walked him to the door.

Alex gave me a hug. "Thank you, my friend, for a fantastic day, and a superlative spaghetti dinner."

"You're ever-and-always welcome, Alex." I returned his hug, and he was gone. I rejoined Mitch on the sofa.

"What was on your mind tonight, sweet girl?" he asked, putting his arm around me.

"Oh, so much …." I thought to tell him about the vision, but I just could not make myself do it. It was very real in my mind, but seemed too ridiculous to say out loud.

"Yeah. Your mom leaving and … everything. There's a lot to contemplate."

I nodded.

"About tomorrow, I'm thinking … what if we went to my section of the underground city? The weather's nice, and, as I said, I think our friends would love it."

"*No!*" I sort of barked. Oh dear, that would never do!

"All … all right." He frowned, and rightly so.

"I'm sorry. I don't know where that came from. I think it just feels like a bit much at the same time that I'm processing Mom's leaving."

"Oh, sure, that makes sense. I thought it might be a good distraction, but maybe it's too much."

I nodded.

"We'll come up with something." He gave me a hug and stood and we walked hand-in-hand to the door. "See you in the morning, Nikki." He hugged me close, kissed my cheek, then ambled down the hall to his own bed.

I closed the door and dragged myself to my room. It had been a lovely, perfect, fun day. But I felt dissatisfied with myself.

There was something, *something*, in all my revolving thoughts that I was missing. But I simply could not get a picture of what that could be.

*   *

Climbing into my pjs, but completely avoiding the mirror, I crawled into bed. Well, at least I was in pajamas if Yumi happened to wake me up in the morning, instead of yesterday's clothes, like I'd been the last two mornings!

When morning came, I was awakened hearing Mom stirring around. Then I heard her soft voice. I guessed she was talking to Dad. I jumped up, changed into leggings and a sweatshirt, and stepped into the hall. Mom stood by the front door, adding another small suitcase to her pile.

"Good morning, Nikki," she greeted me cheerily. "I don't know why I'm taking so much stuff, but at the last minute I thought I might use some of my own teaching materials, and added them to my stash."

"Good idea, Mom. You made some great visuals for kids that have a hard time reading." I saw her look longingly at the piano. "Yeah. The piano is going to miss you …." I tried to sound teasing, but I'm sure it's true. A fine instrument needs to be played.

"Yes. And I will miss it." She sighed deeply, then looked at me. "And I'll miss you!"

"Me too you, Mom." OMG, those tears threatened again. How old was I? Five?

As we stood by the door, I heard the elevator ping, then the doors slid open, followed by a muted rumbling sound, and next, a soft knock at the door.

"Homer," Mom said. She opened the door, and sure enough, there stood Homer with a luggage cart, smiling, but with a sad look in his eyes.

"Ready for departure?" he asked, putting her luggage on the cart.

"As ready as I can be," Mom answered, turning to hug me.

"I'm coming down with you."

"Oh. Okay."

The three of us walked in the jungle-thick carpet back to the elevator. Homer pressed the button, and the doors slid open. We crowded inside with the luggage cart and rode silently down the seven floors to street level. As we stepped out, I saw Mom's Lyft was already at the door.

Not even a few minutes to say good-bye!

Homer taking the lead, went through the front doors and started loading Mom's luggage in the car's trunk. We stood by, wordless. For once!

Mom wrapped her arms around me, and I held her close too. We didn't need to say anything. She kissed my cheek. "I'll text when Dad and I get to the hotel we're temporarily staying in."

"Call, Mom. Call."

"Call?" Mom said, surprised. I'm always telling them to text me.

"Yes. Call."

She nodded, slipped into the back seat, the Lyft pulled away, and she was gone.

I closed my eyes, breathing deeply. Was I up to the challenges at hand?

Was I?

Homer came over and put a friendly hand on my shoulder. "You're not alone, you know."

I smiled at him weakly. "I know, Homer. I know. But we … we've never been apart for more than four days. It's … it's weird to think about. I mean. This is what I wanted, but I don't know what to think!"

"Don't stress yourself, my young friend. It'll all sort out, all on its own. Enjoy your lovely, wonderful friends, and the summer."

I looked around at the thick-as-clouds fog that surrounded us. "What summer?"

"Seattle summer," he clarified.

We went inside and I returned to the apartment. Yumi was apparently still sleeping, and I decided to go back to bed myself.

*　　*

Goodness, do you always sleep in your clothes?" Yumi asked some time later.

I opened my eyes and squinted at her. Boy! I had fallen asleep hard! I glanced at the clock. Almost ten-thirty—I'd slept over four hours since Mom left! "No. I woke up when I heard Mom stirring around, and threw this on to go down with her to the Lyft. I totally crashed out when I came back."

"So she's gone."

"Yeah. I told her to call me when she got to the hotel. They must be there by now."

At that moment, my phone rang. "Here I am, safe and sound," Mom said. "Your dad and I are going to go house hunting today. The hotel is nice, but I don't want to unpack and repack."

Dad took the phone from her. "How's it going, with you two girls there, all alone? Are you okay?"

"Dad, I've been without parents for almost five hours. So far, so good." I chuckled.

"Right. I know, Birdie-Love. But—and I mean this—Do. Not. Hesitate. To. Call."

"I know Dad, I know."

"What are you doing today?"

"We haven't decided yet. Shall I text you when we figure it out?"

"That'd be nice."

"No, dear," I heard Mom's reprimanding voice in the background.

"No. Of course not. Not unless you want to, of course. As long as your Mom was there, I didn't worry about you. But now, of course …."

"Continue as before," I said. I wanted to laugh. But maybe he was picking up on something. "I'll call if there's anything amiss." Already I was lying because *something was amiss*. I just didn't know what.

Chapter X
Sea Creatures

itch and Alex came to the door at the same moment a couple hours later.

"How did you do that?" I asked, after opening the door to them.

"What?" Mitch asked.

"How did you come to the door at the exact same moment?"

"I was at Zingas Grocery, getting some odds and ends for my mother." He held up a Zingas Grocery bag. "Which I have to run down to her. I'll be right back."

"Okay."

Alex and I stood in the doorway, and Mitch came back a minute later. Yumi had joined us, and we all stood, half in the hall, half in the apartment, looking at one another.

"We *could* sit," I suggested

"We could," Alex said, as we moved to the sofas. "Your mom got off, safe and sound?"

"Yes, and she called, and I had to reassure my dad that we were still alive, even though I'd been alone for almost five hours."

Alex chuckled. "You're his little princess!"

"*Uggg*," I gave him a dirty look. "Anyway! What shall we do today?" I glanced out the window. Still foggy. "I'd thought of going up the Space Needle, but with this fog, there's little point."

"That would be fantastic!" Yumi said. "To be up in the fog, high above the city …."

"Even if there's nothing to see?"

"Even if!" She nodded.

"What do you guys think?"

Mitch shrugged like it didn't matter, he was up for anything.

"I like the idea," Alex said. "I've been to the top of the Space Needle on sunny days, but never in fog. Plus, there won't be crowds."

"That's a good point," I agreed. "And then I thought we might go to the aquarium, too, as it's less than a mile from the Space Needle."

"Love it," Mitch said. "I've only been there once, when I was a little kid … with … my dad."

Well, I knew what that meant. Anything he and his deceased father had *done* together was special, and I would do what I could to be sure it stayed special. "Hey! We have a plan! Let's get in motion."

Yumi and I jumped up and scurried off to gather jackets for the chilly day, and backpacks and whatever else we might need, then rejoined Mitch and Alex.

I called for a Lyft and by the time we got to the street our ride was waiting. Soon we all piled out at the foot of the Space Needle, and, as Alex had predicted, there was almost no one there. We zipped up to the top. Despite my conviction that it would not be very interesting with nothing more to see than solid fog, Yumi was right. There was something strange and otherworldly to be in the nearly solid, cottony whiteness.

"It's more interesting than I thought," I said as we gathered close together, staring out an observation window at the whiteness. All alone, just us, in our little group. "Look at all those different shades of white. Pale white, dark white, translucent white, opaque white. White in streams, and white on pillowy pillows. Sooo interesting! You were right, Yumi."

"Yes. More right than I could have guessed. We're inside a giant's mattress!"

We wandered around the observation deck, saying little, encountering no one else. But even as we peered out at white upon white, it began to thin. Before long, we could faintly see the city below, materializing before our very eyes. We could see movement, unable at first to make out details. Then, gradually the vehicles—cars, buses, and trucks—could be seen scurrying about, along with tiny, little, colorful ant-like people, dashing to and fro.

So much like looking at an anthill, which I recalled from my childhood when I happened upon an anthill one afternoon. Getting down on the ground, I watched the ants for an hour, and when I got home very late, I found Mom freaking out, about to call the police.

I told her about the anthill, but she wasn't even able to hear me until the next day when she'd calmed down. That's how protected I was. I hoped and hoped sincerely that I would not cause her any such grief, now that she trusted me, and had no idea where I was, any hour of the day.

"*Wow!*" Alex exclaimed. "Poof, the fog is almost gone!"

"Yeah," Mitch agreed, "pretty fascinating to see the city materialize out of the mist, like magic."

"Ummm," I nodded, taking his hand. "Very mystical. And beautiful!"

We continued to drink in the ever-fading mist until the sun burst through the clouds above, and sunlight radiated everywhere. We wandered again around the whole observation deck, enjoying the city and the surrounding territory, as far as the eye could see.

"It could not have been better in any way," Yumi said as we came back to where we started.

We all agreed, feeling pretty satisfied with ourselves.

"Aquarium?" I asked.

"*Aquarium!*" they chorused.

We rode back down to street level and walked to the aquarium. I tried not to make Yumi uncomfortable by not being as cozy with Mitch as I wanted, which would leave her sort of alone with Alex. *But it wasn't easy!* I wanted to hold his hand. I loved, loved, *loved* holding his hand. I often thought that our hands so perfectly fit together, just the right size, like they belonged together.

But I walked beside Yumi, with Mitch and Alex behind us. We chatted about the city, pointing out things that caught our attention.

When we got to the aquarium, I was able to use my family membership card that let me and a guest in for free, and two other guests for half price. I was completely in my element, being able to play host to my friends.

"Thank you so much," Alex said once we stepped inside. "We'll treat you to lunch!"

"Great idea," Mitch said.

Yumi nodded, "Yes, we must pamper her!"

"No, no, no pampering needed," I protested, lapping it up.

Once inside, we wandered about in wonder, sharing a reverent quietness as we moved among the exhibits. And then we came to the amazing water dome. It always made me feel so tiny when coming under it. Today was no exception—so beautiful and breathtaking – but also a bit scary. As if I'd said this out loud, Mitch came and took my hand. Now, *that* was what I wanted! I'm sorry, Yumi, but you're just going to have to deal with either keeping your distance from Alex by your own devices, or befriend him, I thought.

The subdued blue lighting made us look like mer-people who had lost our lovely tails, but who were still able to be underwater, under the phenomenal dome.

Our mood shifted when we came to the mammals. We laughed at the antics of the seals and sea otters, and even more at the little river otter, interacting with us playfully. Although I felt sorry for him, as he was all alone without another of his kind.

"I do hope the aquarium gets him a little playmate," I said.

"Yeah. Poor little guy," Mitch agreed. "Although he seems happy enough."

"Umm," I replied.

"It would be sad to be the only one of a kind," Yumi said.

"Unless you never knew otherwise," Alex suggested.

"Hmmm, it gets philosophical pretty fast, doesn't it?" I observed.

"It does!" Mitch snuggled closer to me.

Yummy! "No. I would not care to be the only one of a kind."

*   *

"Hungry!" Alex declared as we came to the end of the exhibits. "They have a nice cafe here, shall we stay?"

"Oh, I like that!" I said, not quite ready to leave the blue environment.

"Yes, let's stay here," Yumi agreed.

I was pleased to see her—of her own accord!—standing by Alex, not even trying to move to my side, like she had all day.

Progress—my two friends may yet become friends!

We settled in a corner of the cafe, and my friends brought to me a garden burger, sweet potato fries, and hot tea. A perfect lunch in every way!

"What was your favorite creature?" I asked when we'd settled in.

"He's sort of scary, but I love the octopus," Yumi answered. "I looked at him, and he looked right at me. I mean, he really, truly made eye contact. Sort of shivery to see his intelligence. To realize he really saw me. I wondered, *what are you thinking?*"

"He thought, 'now, there's a cute human,'" Alex said, chuckling.

"No, Alex," I said. "Yumi asked, 'what did the *octopus* think,' not, 'what did *you* think.'"

"Oh!" Alex shrugged. "I'm sure an intelligent octopus is going to think that both of the young women in our group are particularly attractive."

"Nice save," Mitch laughed. "In any case, I agree with the octopus. Or Alex. But to answer your question, Nikki, every creature fills me with awe, but today I was particularly charmed by the little otter. When you pointed out, Nikki, that he is all alone, he got my heart."

"*Awww!*" we all breathed in unison.

"I was taken by the Sculpin," I said, "with their grippy fins kinda like feet so they can hang onto rocks in fast flowing water."

"And that great big head," Mitch said. "He's got lots to think about, I bet."

"What about you, Alex?" I asked.

"Well, I hesitate, because … because, I was the most taken by the octopus, too. But I don't want to sound like I'm saying it because Yumi said it. I watched as the octopus and Yumi made eye contact. I saw it! It was … amazing. Even when Yumi walked away, his eyes followed her. Then I stood in front of him and he made eye contact with *me*—no mistaking it! I had the same thought as Yumi—what is going through your mind, intelligent creature?"

"We should do some research on Mr. Octopus, and see what science has to say about his intelligence," I said.

"Great idea!" Yumi chirped.

*　　*

After lunch, we agreed to take one more turn under the watery dome. It just seemed right to tie up the outing with another few moments of honoring the sea creatures.

Back outside, the sun was pale, and the fog began to roll in again off Puget Sound.

Mitch and I ambled along, comfortably holding hands. I was so relieved that it didn't seem to bother Yumi, who walked ahead of us with Alex. Still keeping her distance, but chatting with him a bit. Yes, I knew she was somewhat uncomfortable. But I could see she wasn't miserable.

The fog began to roll in, in great blankets of dampness. Not quite cold, but I was glad I'd brought my jacket. Few people were about, and we could hear our own muffled footfalls. We meandered without direction, but finally came to the water, listening to it lapping in gentle waves.

"Tide's in," Alex noted.

"It sounds lovely," Yumi said.

We stood silent, transfixed, listening to the lapping water and the remote fog horn, bleak and lonely out there, as if it, too, was the only one of its kind, calling out, longing to find a companion.

"Beautiful, but lonely," Yumi whispered.

"Yes. Beautiful, but lonely." I repeated. "Well, anything else anyone wants to do? Shall we head home?"

"Home," Alex said.

Mitch got out his phone and looked at the time. "Yes. Home. That's a good idea!"

I called for a Lyft, and we headed back toward the street. But I found myself wondering why Mitch checked the time. I think I never saw him do that.

I know, it's completely not a big deal, but still … *strange.*

The Lyft came directly and shuttled us home. One of the other doormen stood at the door, so my plan of giving Homer a brief sketch of our day, which I was sure he'd enjoy, was not to be.

We sprawled out on the sofas and floor like bendy dominos. I realized that we would soon be hungry, and I'd made no plan for a meal.

Once again, Mitch got out his phone and looked at the time. "I'll be right back." He went through the door before I could say a word. But a few moments later, I heard him talking with someone in the hall. Then he came in with his mother, their arms full of pots and pans.

I jumped up off the floor and hurried over to them. "What?...."

"My mother made us dinner! It was completely her idea. Which is why I had to get things from Zingas this morning."

"Oh!" I exclaimed, "Oh!" I said again, a complete sentence eluding me, but insight about Mitch's repeated time-checking suddenly making sense. "But Mrs. Dalca, you needn't have .... " Amazing aromas rose from the steaming dishes they held.

"Of course not. I wanted to. But may we set these down? There's more."

"Of course! Of course!" I led the way to the dining room—getting another good use in such a short while! She and Mitch began to arrange the serving dishes, while Yumi and Alex leapt up and brought dishes and silver and cups and glasses, setting the table. Alex even gathered a few plants from the conservatory.

Mitch and his mother hurried back down the hall to gather yet more goodies.

Stepping out in the hall I called, "Need any help?"

"No. We've got it."

I returned to the dining room to see that Yumi and Alex had done a beautiful job of putting everything in place and were lighting candles.

"Lovely!"

Mitch and his mother came into the dining room, and set the rest of the feast on the sideboard.

We stood around the table as if waiting for some command, I guess.

"Well, let's eat," I said. "But first, Mrs. Dalca, please tell us what you've made with this wonderful surprise."

She began to describe the various Eastern European dishes she'd made for us, lovely varieties of vegetables as I had never imagined. *Ajvar*, roasted bell peppers, and *aubergine*, with paprika and garlic, *tavche grache*, a bean, tomato, and onion stew, and *burek*, filo stuffed with cooked spinach.

And for dessert, *mascota*—I couldn't wait, it sounded so fantastic!—a ganache chocolate and creme with candied orange peel, covered in a thick layer of chocolate. Chocolate with chocolate—speaking my language!

"Thank you so kindly. This is really … words fail me!" I said.

"Well, let's eat, and then thank me, if I still deserve it!"

Oh, did she deserve it!

I had no idea Mitch's mother was such an amazing cook. Chef, really. She explained that she put her own touch to several of the dishes. I don't know what those touches were, but they were *heavenly*.

"You could open a little cafe," I said when I had eaten more than my body weight. Well, nearly. "Really, I'm not exaggerating. You're a stupendous cook. Chef."

"I've told her that, myself, many times," Mitch said, beaming. "She didn't do much cooking when … when we were under the oppression of my uncle. But she's been getting back into it. I was so happy when she said she wanted to do this for us. With the same cultural background as Zingas Grocery, they carry many of the more esoteric items."

"Oh! You mean that strange rack with the fascinating little bottles and tins, and everything in a language unknown to me, that I've stood before many times, wondering what their contents might be?"

"Yes," Mitch said. "That very rack."

There was a resounding knock at the door. We all stopped, silent as the fog.

"Who could that be?" I wondered aloud.

"Why not go to the door and find out," Mitch's mother suggested.

"All right. I will. Don't anyone go anywhere."

I went to the door, while the dining room remained silent, as everyone listened attentively. It was true that no one, and I mean no one, ever came to our doors without our knowing it, with the ever-present and faithful Homer and his cohorts.

And … speaking of whom, I opened the door to … *Homer!*

"Hi, Nikki. I had the afternoon off and just wanted to see your cheerful smile. Making sure everything is all right."

"Everything is wonderful, Homer. Everything is …." And then a brilliant—and obvious—idea sprung to mind. "In fact, as you're 'off duty,' you must join us."

"Oh, no, Nikki, I wouldn't think of intruding on you young folks."

"Well, we're not all young folks. I mean, we're not old folks, either. I mean, oh, phooey, just please, stop standing in the hall and come inside!"

I tugged on his sleeve, and, somewhat reluctantly, he stepped inside.

"Follow me!" Not taking no for an answer, I led him into the candlelit, smiling faces realm of the dining room.

"Oh! Oh my goodness!" He looked around the room, taking each of my guests in, in turn, and finally seeing Mitch's mother. "Well, now, this is a sight! So very good to see you, Mrs. Dalca."

"And you, Homer."

"She made this amazing dinner for us! A complete surprise! It's unbelievable, and I insist you join us."

"Yes, yes, please, Homer, sit down," everyone called.

"Here's a chair, just for you, as you can see," Mitch said, pointing out the sixth, and empty, chair.

"Well, well, really, I shouldn't, I don't know if it's quite professional."

"Phooey to professional!" I protested. "You're off duty. You're our friend. We're inviting you to dinner. We're going to tell you about our fantastic day!"

"All right, then. All right." He moved around the table and sat in the vacant—just for him!—chair.

For some reason, this made us all burst into cheers.

We loved our Homer!!

We regaled him and Mitch's mother with lengthy and detailed stories of our day. How had we done so much? I was stunned just listening to each story, told from my friends' hearts.

The food, the candlelight, the warmth, the love, it just … completely filled up the room and spilled out into the hall.

And that was not all.

I may be young, but I'm observant. As I watched everyone, feeling quite emotional about everything, I noted glances from Homer to Mitch's mom. And why not? She's an exotically beautiful woman. Much more now than I had noticed before. She had blossomed in the absence of the tyrant, Mitch's uncle.

Of course, any adult man would give Mitch's mother more than a glance.

But here's what took my attention.

Mitch's mother *gave many of those glances from Homer—back to him!* Romance in the air? Wouldn't that be *toooo* sweet? I could claim to have had something to do with it. Yes. Because I was a needy little waif, all alone and parentless, who must have adults look after me.

Yep.

Perhaps I was the matchmaker!

Chapter XI
Great Aunt Meechie

Our dinner could not have been more perfect. After we'd all eaten until we practically burst, Mitch's mother and Homer left—that is to say, Mitch's mother said she was "going to leave the young people to themselves," and Homer insisted on "walking her home."

A-hem! Yes … well … ask no questions and be told no lies!

The four of us continued to sit around the dining room table. Everyone too lazy to get up and clear things away, we continued to pick at the delicious bits still on the table, as the candles burned down lower and lower.

I was in a cocoon of cozy, when Mitch shocked me out of my reverie by bringing up a subject I would have imagined he'd confirm with me first. Disconcerting in every way!

"So… I've taken Nikki to a place that I discovered, that I think we might all enjoy going to tomorrow. It needs to remain secret, for reasons you'll see. I don't want people to trammel it into oblivion. Are you up for it?"

"Well, as I have no idea what you're talking about I guess I'll say a tentative yes," Yumi said.

"I'm game," Alex agreed on the heels of Yumi's tentative affirmation.

Mitch's gaze finally rested on me, and the big smile on his face faded as he took in my look, which, even in candlelight, I'm sure registered shock and disapproval.

"Well … maybe not …."

"I … it's … fine," I finally said. Rock, meet hard place. I would only sound like an ogre if I resisted. And, anyway, I felt certain I'd be out-voted.

Sometimes one had to simply give everything up to Fate, and hope that Fate's plan was a good one.

"So … what is it, Nikki!" Yumi asked.

"I cannot tell. That is to say, I could, but it's not mine to tell. Tomorrow will unfold in its own telling," I said ominously. I tried to sound sort of melodramatic. But there was truth under the melodrama.

"Well, then, I don't know …." Yumi said hesitantly. "Maybe it's something we ought to let the guys do, and we'll just stay here and entertain ourselves."

"But …." Mitch looked at me again, clearly bemused by my resistance. "Really, Yumi, it's because of something you said, something you've liked, that I'd like to share my discovery."

Yumi looked at me again.

I shrugged. I would do what I could to protect my friends come the next day. In the meantime … in the meantime, I faced this after-dinner mess that needed to be cleaned up!

As if reading my mind, and surely wanting to turn me from unhappy to happy, Mitch said, "Okay, Alex, my friend, let's clean up the disarray in here. You two young ladies stay right where you are. Don't lift a finger!"

"Suits me fine," I said, leaning back, sipping my water.

"Me too!" Yumi giggled, imitating me.

Mitch and Alex bustled about as if clearing tables was something they did every day.

Mitch called to me from the kitchen, "I'll put the leftovers in plastic containers, and we can have them for a nice lunch tomorrow."

"Good idea," I called back, too ensconced to even get up and show him where the plastic containers were. He'd find them.

There ensued noisy thrashing about, and he finally called, "Found the containers!"

I looked at Yumi, "I knew he would."

"Tell me what this thing is tomorrow," she whispered, "so I can be prepared. How should I dress? Is it not nice, somehow?"

"Wear jeans and shoes for hiking. It's … fascinating, but … well, more I dare not say. You'll have to badger Mitch if you must know more."

"Badgering is not a part of my skill set," Yumi said, making me laugh outright.

"No. It's not. You're entirely too refined for badgering."

Mitch stepped into the room, happy to see me laughing. "What's funny?"

"Yumi was asking me to tell her about where you're taking us, and I said she'd have to badger you about it, to which she replied that badgering is not a part of her skill set."

"True," Mitch agreed. "You're too … mannerly for badgering."

"I said, 'refined.'"

"That too." He gathered up the last of the dishes and carried them to the kitchen. I soon heard the dishwasher swishing away. The dining room was in perfect order, while one of the candles began to sputter, coming to the end of its wick. Out its light went. And still, I loathed to get up.

Mitch and Alex returned. "Everything is cleaned and put away," Mitch said. "I'll collect my mother's pots and pans tomorrow." He came over and kissed me on the forehead. "See you in the morning, Nikki. Don't worry, everything will be great!"

"'Night, Yumi, Nikki," Alex said.

"Good night," Yumi answered softly.

The two of them left us in the near-darkness of the single candle.

"What a lovely evening," Yumi finally said.

"Yes," I agreed, not quite wholeheartedly. "I had no idea Mitch's mother was such an amazing cook. Truly amazing."

"She is."

Without preamble or segue, it came to me to ask Yumi the question I'd been burning to ask her. This might not be the right moment, but I plowed ahead. "So … I was reading something lately," I half-lied, "and I encountered a name. I was wondering if it's a Japanese name. It's 'Meechie.'"

"Oh, yes, a girl's name, yes. Goodness, what a coincidence! It was my great, or great-great, or great-great-great Aunt's name. I honestly do not know how many greats.

"But after my mom agreed that I could stay with you this summer, she told me—and I never knew this before—that my however many greats aunt Meechie had lived here. She said the family emigrated to Seattle way back in the mid-eighteen hundreds.

"I've been going to tell you, but it just slipped my mind. This aunt was a milliner. She apparently made a name for herself and became wealthy. Her sister, my great-great, however many greats grandmother met her husband-to-be, got married, then moved to Southern California. But Aunt Meechie never married. She stayed single, making lots of money and having influential customers. How strange that you ask me about that name."

"Strange. Yes. Surprising coincidence …. interesting…." And while interesting, it was considerably more than strange.

Yumi stifled a yawn and stood. "Well, I'm off to bed. I'm exhausted. Are you going?"

"In a few. Think I'll keep this little candle company."

"Okay. See you in the morning."

"See you. Sleep sweet."

I didn't get up and go to bed because I knew I had to … *had to* … look in the mirror to see if it would tell me more than it had before. And I was in no frame of mind to see bad news. If only the mirror would show my friends not disappearing when they got to that room!

The solution, of course, was to stick to them like a burr, not letting them out of my sight. Whatever else I did or did not do, *whatever else—I would not let them enter that room!*

*　　*

Fairly soon the little candle joined its mate and winked out. I could no longer put off the inevitable. I got up, and, closing the dining room door quietly behind me, went to my room. Then, like ripping a band-aid off, I stepped into my closet and stood before the mirror. Somewhat challengingly, I must admit.

But nothing appeared. Though I stood there, angry and frightened, I saw nothing other than myself—looking angry and frightened.

I finally turned away, changed into my flannel pjs and crawled into bed, tumbling into sleep, wondering what the next day held.

Chapter XII
Millie's Millinery

I woke up the next morning to my phone pinging. It was Mitch, texting his concern about my disapproval the night before. I glanced out the window, and it was, again, a beautiful, sunny day. My fears of the previous evening seemed a bit small and silly.

"Not to worry," I texted back. "Everything will be fine."

I jumped up, showered, then pulled on jeans and a tee-shirt, layered it with a sweatshirt depicting the Space Needle and got out my hiking boots.

I put a flashlight and a few other "must have" items in my backpack and hurried out, ready to run to the conservatory and get Yumi up, but she was already in the kitchen, dressed and ready to go, calmly enjoying a cup of tea.

"You're up!"

"Yes. And cautiously ready for a day of mysterious adventure."

"Good." I thrashed through the refrigerator, studying all the neatly stacked leftovers from the night before. "I'll pack this food in a picnic basket to take with us. I'm sure it'll be tasty even if not heated up."

"Especially if we're hungry!" Yumi agreed.

My phone pinged again. "Ready?" Mitch texted.

"Yep. Just packing up the food to take with us."

"Great! I'll be right there."

I let him in and he followed me back into the kitchen. I got out the picnic basket, and we put everything in it we could possibly want, excluding, we agreed, the kitchen sink.

Yumi watched us orchestrate the food. "What teamwork!"

"Why, thank you. Completely spontaneous, and without rehearsal," I replied.

"Okay, let's go," Mitch urged. "Alex is waiting for us at the grocery store."

Yumi and I gathered our backpacks, and we were soon on the elevator, riding down to the street and stepping out the back door to the parking garage. We made our way to Mitch's big, old, Chevy that had become his when his uncle was sent to prison. Out of habit, I jumped in the front beside Mitch. Then I realized that that would leave Yumi in the back with Alex.

I looked back at her. "Are you okay back there, you know, with …?"

She nodded. "I'll be fine. He hasn't bitten me yet."

"And not likely too," Mitch said, smiling at her in the rearview mirror.

"I hope you're right."

Alex waited for us outside his dad's grocery, pacing back and forth. "Finally! I was afraid a big order would come in and Dad would ask me to deliver it 'quickly' like he always says, and you'd have to wait for me. You would wait for me, yes?"

"Maybe," I said, teasing. Of course, we'd wait for him!

All together now, we were finally on the road. We drove through the city and eventually came to green hillsides and trees.

"How *beautiful*," Yumi sighed. She and Alex had said nothing more than "hi" since he got in.

"It *is* beautiful," I agreed. Still, there was little conversation from anyone, as we all anticipated the near-known—or unknown—future.

For my part, I could not take my mind off what Yumi had told me the night before about her Great Aunt. It seemed that Millie, or Meechie, must certainly be one and the same person. After all, how many Japanese milliners named Meechie, or Millie, were there likely to be in Seattle in the eighteen hundreds? Probable answer: one.

Finally, we came to the quiet knoll under which lay Mitch's secret discovery. He pulled onto the little hill, turned off the engine, and we all climbed out.

"So … where are we?" Alex asked.

"Follow me," Mitch led the way without looking back. It soon appeared as though he disappeared into the earth.

"*What?!*" Yumi exclaimed.

Alex, getting a clue, hurried after Mitch, and I followed.

"Coming!" Yumi called as she scurried after me.

I stepped down the first step, then the second into the earth that Mitch had carved out when he'd discovered this part of the underground city.

I took the third and the fourth step. I saw the shadow of Yumi above me. "What are we doing?" she called.

"Just take that first step down, then you'll see the rest."

She took a step down, and I took another step down, reminding myself that the only thing I'd promised myself is that I'd stick to my friends like a burr, and we were already all spread out. On the one hand, it might be better if Yumi didn't come down. But, on the other, she would eventually, and the best thing I could hope for at the moment was to get us all together. I took another step down, and glanced at Millie's billboard.

It immediately began to change. Millie's features shifted into the delicate Japanese beauty I'd seen in the mirror. The letters on the billboard slid about crazily, and in moments, it said *Meechie's Millinery*. Millie—or Meechie—for the first time in forever, stopped gazing up at the sky. She looked down at me.

Whatever was about to transpire, it was upon me. Then I saw movement at the top of the stairs. And there, *there* was that green-eyed, gray-striped little cat! She trotted down the stairs and jumped on the boardwalk, glancing back at me. *"Come along!"* her look urged.

I looked around for Yumi, but she had apparently passed me by while I was entranced with Meechie. Millie was once again looking up at the sky.

I heard Yumi's voice faintly, far ahead of me, along with a reply from Mitch, on the boardwalk.

Bad news! They were all far ahead of me in the bowels of the underground city. I got out my flashlight and hurried after the little gray-striped cat, calling to my friends, who, so busy chatting among themselves, did not seem to hear me. I had to hurry, but I also had to move carefully. It would not be helpful to fall off the boardwalk or otherwise take a misstep.

As I scurried, the cat stayed the same distance ahead of me, not pausing, and simply not letting me stop—not that I intended to. I seemed to be getting closer. I heard their voices a bit louder. Then I heard them climbing steps.

"No! Don't go into that house!" I called.

But they didn't hear me. Before long, the cat was running up the porch steps, and I followed her. Yes, this familiar house! I went through the front door. I heard Alex asking a question, muffled and sounding like he was farther away than in the next room. I passed through the next room, and the next, now hearing nothing from my friends.

My heart pounded. I couldn't think about ... what if they ... no. Couldn't think about it. The floor creaked and sort of gave a bit underfoot. I moved more cautiously. The cat slinked through the next ornate door, just barely ajar. As I stepped into the darkness, the cat disappeared.

Breathing heavily, I wondered what to do. I waved my flashlight crazily about the room, and there my three friends stood at the window, with that amazingly completely intact with unbroken glass. Just as I'd seen in the vision. They stood around the window as if looking out at a sunny day.

Mitch flashed his light on my face. "What's wrong?" he asked, no doubt seeing the terror written on my features.

"Oh. You're all here. I thought … I was … I mean … thank goodness, you're all here."

"Yes. Here we are. Where else would we be?"

"I … I'm not too sure. Why were you all so quiet?"

"Yumi came over to this window and asked us to imagine what it must have been like to look out this window and see the world as it was when this house was above ground," Alex said. "And we were … we were doing that. Sort of a bit in a trance, I think."

Yumi came to me and put her arm around me. "Goodness, you're white as a ghost!"

"Don't say that!" I exclaimed.

"I'm sorry if we frightened you. You were so engaged in looking at that beautiful billboard on the stairs, I didn't want to disturb you."

"All right, all right!" I said, calming down. Then I looked around for the cat. "Did you see the cat? Where did that cat go?"

"What cat?" Mitch asked.

"The little gray cat with the green eyes."

"You and gray cats!" Yumi laughed. "Maybe she's your familiar."

"Oh! Ohhh!" Maybe she was! And then I had a great *aha!* that, astounding though it may be, I could not share with my friends.

It wasn't my friends who would disappear, it was the little cat who would disappear when I was on the right track. And now I knew….

There was something in this room I was supposed to know about, or to find or … or … something. But I would not discover it while I was here with everyone. The mirror would show the unfolding of fate in due time.

I let out a huge sigh of relief. Realizing that my friends were safe, I was now in the mood! "Let's explore," I practically crowed, my feelings shifting from ominous to curious.

And explore we did! We crept back through the house and down the stairs, and then went further into the underground city than I had ever gone, sending the light of our flashlights over the fronts of Victorian houses, sleeping peacefully in their underground terrain.

"I'm hungry!" Mitch finally said.

In unanimous agreement, we retraced our path and came up out of the ground like a bunch of moles, blinking and squinting in the bright afternoon sunlight.

I pointedly *did not* look at Millie's billboard.

It didn't take us long to spread out a blanket and the great feast contained in the picnic basket, soon devouring what was left of Mitch's mother's amazing meal.

Chapter XIII
Follow the Cat!

Yumi couldn't stop practically raving about Mitch's underground city.

"It's so amazing, Mitch! Much more remarkable than the tour downtown. You could make a fortune!"

Mitch looked at me with a, "Have I created a monster?" look.

I shrugged. It was your decision to do this without talking to me, and you must suffer the consequences, my reply look said. Well, I tried to convey a look that said that. I believe he got the gist.

For myself, I was simply delighted that I resurfaced on terra firma with the same number of friends with which I'd entered the bowels of the earth.

"First of all, Yumi," Mitch started to lecture, "no, I can't make a fortune. I don't own this land."

"Oh. True," Yumi acquiesced. "I didn't think of that."

"I looked up the owner, they live off in that direction." He waved vaguely. "Technically, we're completely trespassing.

"But secondly, if I *did* own the land, I would never have a tour 'to make a fortune.' I don't need a fortune. Fortunes are entirely over-rated. I say that from first-hand observation of family members who amassed fortunes, only to see them miserable and immoral, doing all they could to increase their fortunes, never doing anything worthwhile. The only reason I might consider a fortune to be a good thing, is if I could help people, or animals, or the planet.

"But, more to the point, I wouldn't turn this amazing historical site into a tour because it's too precious. It wouldn't take long before that this stunning bit of history would be destroyed."

"True, true and true," Yumi agreed. "I didn't think it through." She looked at me. "You have a very wise boyfriend."

"I know!" I agreed, finishing off the last of the baked root veggies—a rutabaga I think. "But, Yumi, you can't tell anyone about this place."

"Oh! Not even my mother?"

"Not even. Maybe especially. What do you think your mother would think … or say … or even *do*, if she knew you had climbed down some dirt steps into the earth, and wandered around in a place that, quite frankly, could be dangerous?"

"Dangerous?"

"Well, sure. Victorian era homes, underground—there could be a cave-in. The houses can't be very strong or stable. The boardwalk could give way. It's not a kids' playground."

"Where," Alex pointed out, "kids get badly hurt, every day."

I turned to look at him.

"Okay. That, too," I said, feeling we'd gotten a bit off-topic. "Anyway, Yumi, you are sworn to secrecy. Sworn! You must honor Mitch's trust in you, and protect his discovery."

"All right, all right," Yumi begrudgingly agreed. "But you know, Nikki, I tell my mother everything."

"Except this."

"Except this. Which is *HUGE!*"

"Regardless …." I said firmly. I looked at Mitch, who had remained strangely silent.

"Well, I'm now very sorry to have caused this conflict." I'd never heard this tone of voice from him, nor had I ever seen this expression on his face. He seemed, somehow, beaten.

Yumi picked right up on it. "No! *No-no-no*, Mitch! Please, do not be sorry. I'm so … so touched that you trusted me with your precious secret. No. No conflict. I'm … well, I'm just silly! I'm a young adult, and I could at least pretend to behave like one. Goodness, speaking of princesses!

"You're such a lovely person, Mitch." She reached over and gave him a little hug. "A lovely young man, when I've been hating men. And you … you've put my faith and my trust back in the gender. I mean, the possibility that men are not all conniving and horrible."

"Well," Mitch smiled that adorably crooked smile of his when something bemused him. "I guess that's a compliment."

"Oh, my! I'm just digging in deeper." Yumi sighed. "I am now going to shut up and eat."

"There's a great bumper sticker," I laughed. "'*Shut Up and Eat!*"

We all had a great laugh and then, well, we shut up and ate.

*   *

After eating everything we'd brought with us, we sprawled on the blanket, soporific. Alex stretched on one edge of the blanket, and actually fell asleep.

Yumi wandered back down the stairs, to, she said, contemplate Millie's billboard, promising to not go all the way down alone. And, much to my complete contentment, Mitch lay down with his head in my lap. We chatted about nothing consequential, while I twirled his beautiful black hair with my fingers.

Finally he said, "I really did do wrong to spring coming here on you without talking to you about it first."

"No. 'Wrong' would be ... wrong. But, it did surprise me that you didn't even mention it to me. I don't know. What's 'right,' what's 'wrong' in a relationship? We're young. It's all new to both of us. What I see of my parents is, it seems like they talk about everything. But then again, I don't know. Maybe they both have deep, dark secrets that nobody knows about."

"Seems unlikely," Mitch noted.

"Yes. It does. But, anyway, how will it feel if you think you 'have to' share everything with me? If you don't simply spontaneously want to, then, surely that would damage a relationship."

"But, Nikki, I do tell you everything. Because I want to. Ahm, that's to say, I tell you everything, even the unpleasant stuff, because if I don't, it'll get in the way someday, sometime. But this, this was about my wanting to surprise you with something fun. I wanted to show you that I trust your friend."

"I know. I understand." I did know, and now, I understood. "All that matters is that all's well that ends well. And this has."

"So it has," Mitch agreed, reaching up to kiss me.

*   *

Dusk had fallen by the time we decided to head back home. Alex suggested we come in to Zingas Grocery when we dropped him off. So we parked the car and piled into the little store, just as Alex's dad was getting ready to close up shop.

"What have you kids been up to all day?" he asked.

"Oh, ah …." I gave Alex an evil-eye glance. This was his nefarious plan, to have one of us explain the day without giving away what we'd actually done, so that he wouldn't have to make something up to tell his father. "We drove out to the countryside and found a picture-perfect hillside where we had the most spectacular picnic of leftovers from the surprise meal Mitch's mom made for us yesterday," I said, every word of it true.

"Ah, yes, she came in yesterday afternoon to get something Mitch had forgotten, and said something about cooking up a surprise for our favorite young people."

"Even cold, it was amazing. I had no idea she could cook like that!"

"She really outdid herself," Mitch agreed. "She's back to her old self—before … before my dad passed."

Mr. Zingas gave him a sad look. "Sorry, my lad. But I'm happy to hear of your mother's culinary talent. I must say she's looking fantastic!"

"Watch it, Dad," Alex warned. "You're a married man."

"And happily so, my son! Happily so! You mother takes no back seat to anyone. Well, since you ate so heartily on a hillside, I don't suppose you're at all interested in this Hungarian Mushroom soup I have here."

"Oh, boy!" Alex exclaimed. "My favorite! Well, Dad, it's been a good four hours since we ate. I'm sure it's time to eat again."

I nodded. Not that I was particularly hungry, but it was past dinnertime, and it'd be great not to have to think about making supper.

"Sort of perfect, Mr. Zingas," I said. "A light supper after an invigorating day outdoors."

Pouring out bowls of soup, and adding a tray of fancy crackers, Mr. Zingas regaled us with stories of the day's customers.

I was proud of my two friends, especially Yumi, to not make the tiniest slip in reference to our day's activities. After we'd downed the generous soup and crackers, Mitch and Yumi and I piled into Mitch's car and drove the short distance to the parking structure of home.

Yumi went into the apartment while I lingered in the hall with Mitch. A long kiss, and a promise to see one another the next day. I watched as Mitch walked down the hall to his apartment.

Oh, yes. Gorgeous.

He turned and waved, then disappeared inside.

Yumi stood stretching in the foyer.

"Hot chocolate?" I asked.

"Oh, I don't think so. All that fresh air exhausted me!"

Me too, actually. "All right. See you in the morning." I gave her a hug and went to bed.

But I woke up in the night. Something had disturbed me. What was it? A dream? A sound? What? I looked at the clock. Two a.m. Frowning, I tried to imagine why I was wide awake after only a few hours' sleep. I looked at my phone to see if a text had come in.

Nothing. I rolled over, and tried to fall back to sleep, and then I heard what must have awakened me. A muffled, sad, sound.

I slipped out of bed and stood in my bedroom doorway. Oh! It almost sounded like crying. I tiptoed down the hall to the conservatory. The sound stopped, but then started again, and, yes, it sounded like Yumi was crying. Again? *Why?*

Had she not had a lovely day? Several lovely days, in fact. Was it Gary again? Was she homesick? It was true that she and her mother were very, very close, there only being the two of them since her mom divorced her dad when Yumi was five.

I tried to turn and leave her alone in her grief—but, no, I couldn't. My friend was hurting, and I needed to try to comfort her. I stepped into the conservatory.

"Yumi?"

"Ye … yes," she sobbed.

I hurried to her side. "What's wrong? Oh, Yumi, what's the matter?"

She held up her phone. "I just got off the phone with my mother, and … *oh men! They are so horrible!*"

"What happened?" My mind raced. "What happened?"

"Her partner, you know, Ervin, who she has made into who he is. Supposedly her best friend and partner for ten years … ripped her off!"

"What do you mean?"

"He took every cent out of the company account. *Every cent!*"

"Oh! Oh, no. It can't be!" Shocked, I sat on the floor by the bed. I've known Ervin for ten years, myself. I couldn't picture it. "It cannot be!" I said again, unable to imagine any other thing to say. "Surely there's some mistake somehow, somewhere."

"Yes?" Yumi sounded sarcastic. "How is it a mistake that an account is empty of funds and, and that's not the worst part …." Yumi burst into tears again, unable to speak.

"What's worse? What could be worse? Yumi, what's worse?"

"*He stole her designs.* He stole all her fall line designs, which, thankfully, has already been created. But he also took her next spring line. That amazing line of creation that I told you about, so utterly unique. And, I mean, he didn't just take it, he completely erased it from my mother's database and the cloud.

"He knew what he was doing. But why? *Why?*"

I thought fast—if he wanted to claim the designs for himself, he'd have to make sure that they were nowhere in Yumi's mother's world. He would claim the designs were his, and that she tried to steal them from *him*. I refrained from voicing this insight. Yumi didn't need to process more at the moment.

"This is truly terrible," I whispered. "Does she want you to come home?"

"No. And that's another terrible part. Not only did she say, 'do not come home,' which hurts like … hurts so bad, but she said she couldn't pay for a ticket even if she did want me to come home. Which, she said again, she didn't want."

"Well, she can't be alone at a time like this. I'll call Mom and have her go be with her."

"No, Nikki. She specifically said she does not want you to do that. She knew you'd say that, of course. My mom is like that. When things go wrong, she just shuts down. She thinks things through. She doesn't want to be around anyone else. I know that about her. But this exclusion has never included me."

"I will buy you a ticket home, of course, Yumi. Of course!" I reached up and hugged her.

"Thank you, Nikki. All right, if I feel I must go home, I'll be grateful for your generosity. I'll pay you back, of course."

"Oh, hush! You know better than that!"

"But, anyway, since she was so adamant that I not come home, I think I'd better just … stay here. Oh, but I'll make you so miserable with my misery."

"Don't think about that. We have to figure out a way to solve this problem. Anyway, the authorities will surely do something about the embezzlement."

"I don't know, Nikki. Mother seems to feel that she has small chance to recover anything. First of all, the authorities have already traced Ervin having bought a series of airline tickets that have him nearly unfindable. And secondly, she gave him complete and equal access to the company funds, as if they were his. I never knew that until now. So, even if they caught him, Mother says her case would be weak."

"There's a solution. We won't let your mother go down like this." It was strange, how confident I felt that there was a solution, though I knew less than nothing about the business world.

"I'm going to bring a sleeping bag and pillows in here. We'll brainstorm. I know there's a solution." I jumped up and scurried about, grabbing my sleeping bag from the hall closet and my pillows from my bed, and coming back into the conservatory. I moved a few plants that were by Yumi's bed and made a little bed of my own.

Yumi watched me without comment. I was glad she had stopped the heartbreaking sobbing. Maybe she really did count on me to come up with a solution. Well, I would do everything in my power. Yumi and her mother were family to me. I was sorry that her mother wouldn't let Mom at least just be with her. They could maybe brainstorm too, and were likely to come up with better alternatives than I would. But we had to honor her request.

I sat on the makeshift bed I'd made, and Yumi sat on the rollaway, and we chatted. Not so much about ways we might solve the problem as recalling the greatest of her mother's designs. We each brought to mind specific garments we loved. As the sun began to make an appearance through the leaves of the plants, Yumi fell into a troubled sleep.

My phone, which I'd brought with me just in case Yumi thought I should call Mom after all, pinged. It was a text from Mitch.

"Good morning, Beautiful Girl! Just got a call from the attorney's office I've got the internship with—asked me if I could come in today for 'trial run' and orientation. Short notice, but I said yes. I'll call or text later, & let you know what's up. Love You! M."

Curious timing but just as well, as I needed to devote my attention to Yumi.

I was wide awake now, even with only a bit of sleep, and decided to take advantage of Yumi's fitful sleep to get dressed and humanize myself, in order to face whatever had to be faced today.

I scurried down the hall, brushed my teeth, ran a brush through my hair, stepped into my closet to gather something to wear when, completely not anticipating it, the mirror was stirring and roiling about as I had never seen it.

I stopped. I gave it my undivided attention.

Form began to rise.

I closed the closet door. Up through the sepia and silver-golden tones floated Millie's billboard, just exactly as it had appeared to everyone yesterday.

And then it began to change into how only I had seen it yesterday. Millie's face shifted into Meechie's beautiful features. And, for the first time ever, her mouth moved. She was trying to tell me something. Could I hear her? I don't know if I heard her, or just understood her.

"Follow the cat," she said.

Follow the cat.

Again, I sensed movement in the lower right corner of the mirror. Looking down, sure enough, there was the little gray and white-striped, green-eyed, cat. She trotted down the dirt stairs and onto the boardwalk. As if in a movie, I was taken along, following her. Finally, she stepped up onto the porch of the house we'd entered yesterday. She took me to the room we were in when we stood by the intact window imagining a time long gone.

The little cat stopped in the middle of the room. Then she scratched at the floorboards. I noticed, now, that this was the same spot I'd been shown before. There was a small bump in the flooring. The cat scratched at that bump, and the flooring gave way, just a little. A golden light came up along the edges of the board. Kitty pulled at it.

What? *What?!?*

I knew what, yes *I did!* Suddenly, everything fell into place.

I flung on clothes—and dashed to the conservatory, shaking Yumi awake.

Chapter XIV
A Miracle!

"Wake up! Wake up, Yumi. A miracle. A miracle is about to transpire."

"Wha … what?" In her foggy sleepiness, I watched as the memory of why we were up all night crashed back on her. "Oh, Nikki, couldn't you have let me mercifully sleep for a little while?"

"No. I mean, well, *no!* Get up. Throw clothes on. You have your driver's license now, right? And you have it with you?"

"Yes."

"Great. 'Cause I still only have my learner's permit. Get dressed, come on. I have to gather some things. Hurry up!"

I dashed out of the conservatory and thrashed through Dad's cupboard where he had a few—not many, but a few—tools, and a nice little toolbox. I threw in screwdrivers, the hammer, and, *yay!* he had a little crowbar.

"I'm ready," I called, standing by the door. Yumi didn't come and I went back to the conservatory.

She stood by the bed, dressed in yesterday's clothes, looking rumpled and confused.

"Good enough, get your license."

"Right here, in my backpack."

"Excellent." I dragged her to the door. I made her pull on her hiking boots, still by the door with yesterday's dirt on them, while I pulled on mine. We were soon in the parking lot standing by my mom's car. I handed Yumi the car keys. "You must drive."

"*Nikki! Stop!* What are you doing? Where are we going?"

"You won't believe it until you see it. And, anyway, it's too hard to explain. But trust me, I'm absolutely certain I'm about to make you very happy."

"Seems improbable." But without further argument, she took the keys and got in the driver's seat. I ran around the car and jumped in.

"Just go where I say."

"Of course. What else would I do?"

She started the engine and pulled out of the parking structure. I proceeded to tell her where to go. It wasn't long before she recognized where we were headed. "Look, Nikki, I enjoyed yesterday, but going there again is not going to make me happy right now. My mother's life, and well, mine too, are just too overwhelming. I appreciate the thought, I guess. But, really …."

"Just … trust me."

"Right." Yumi gave up trying to reason with me. Which I appreciated.

Finally the grassy little hillside came into view. And why did it take so long? It seemed much longer than when we came here yesterday.

"Park where we were yesterday."

"Right. But, Nikki, I'm not getting out of the car."

"Yes, Yumi, you are. I need your help. I don't think I can do this alone. Anyway, you have to see what I'm about to show you with your own eyes."

I got out, retrieved the tools from the back and stood impatiently while Yumi reluctantly pulled herself from the car as if it was the most difficult thing she'd ever done.

I grabbed her hand and hurried to the dirt stairs. Down we went to the boardwalk. No gray-striped, green-eyed cat this time. Not necessary! She'd already shown me where I was going and what I must do. I flipped on my flashlight and we walked carefully into the depths of darkness.

"Spooky, Nikki. It doesn't feel like it did yesterday."

"That's just ... because of your mood right now." We finally came to "the" house. I went up the porch stairs and looked back down at Yumi, who had not followed.

"You said it might be dangerous. You said there might be a cave in. You said these Victorian houses are not safe."

"I did. But come along now." I waited impatiently for her to join me. Honestly, if she refused, I could not carry her. I felt vexed about what to do if she continued to set her heels in.

But, slowly, she put one foot, then the next, on the stairs, reluctantly joining me. I put the toolbox and flashlight in one hand, and grabbed her hand with the other. "Pay attention now, Yumi. Don't drag your feet."

We went through the first room, then the second, then the third. I released Yumi's hand and put the toolbox down, playing the flashlight over the floorboards, peering intently for that bump. What if it wasn't really here?

No. It was here. I *knew* it. And … there! *There it was!* I took the toolbox to the spot. "I wish I had another flashlight."

"I still have mine in my backpack, from yesterday," Yumi said.

"Well then, bring it here, and shine it on this bump in the flooring." I waved my flashlight around on the bump, then set my flashlight on the floor, shining on the spot.

Yumi thrashed through her backpack, retrieved her flashlight and turned it on the spot I now hovered over, as I got the hammer and screwdriver and crowbar out of the toolbox.

"*What are you doing?*" Yumi said, coming to stand by me.

"Giving you what is yours, I'm pretty sure." I hammered the screwdriver into the edge of the flooring, prying it up and moving it along, prying it up. It wasn't easy, but finally, I had enough of an edge that I could wrangle the crowbar into it.

I leaned on it with all my strength. The ancient and rusted nails gave an unholy screech, but I persisted.

"Nikki, you're acting crazy. Why are you tearing this house apart? Why?"

"Not. Crazy," I emphasized, leaning on the crowbar. *"Not," I pushed! "Crazy!"* I repeated as the floorboard began to give. And then, hinges became exposed, on the back of the strip of floorboard. The two feet of wood flopped back onto the floor.

"You're sure acting cra …." Yumi shined the light into the hole. "O.M.G. Nikki, there's something in there."

"Well, yes, Yumi, *I know that!* You know, I know that!" I reached in and tugged on a black metal box wedged into the space. It was incredibly heavy. I had to sit down on the floor, straddle my legs over the hole and wrench it up, with all my might.

"I hope it's not locked." I tugged on the lid. It did not budge. I shined the flashlight around in the hole in the floor, but saw no key.

"Look on the bottom of the box," Yumi said, with a stunning flash of insight.

I put the box on the floor and rolled it over. How Yumi knew to look there, I don't know, but there was a little metal sort of envelope attached to the bottom of the box, which readily opened. Inside was a key.

"Well, that doesn't seem very practical," I said, thinking it very strange to attach a key to the very item it opened, even though I was glad to see a key. However, when I tried to fit it in the lock, it was entirely the wrong shape and a bit too big.

I glanced around, wondering what to do now. And then, the little gray-striped cat, completely translucent and ghost-like, came through the room and stood by the window with the intact glass, looking at the wall in front of her. Then she faded into nothing.

That's when I noticed that the wallpaper had peeled away under the window frame. I jumped up and scurried over to it. Gently I pulled the ancient, Victorian flowered wallpaper back—exposing something that looked a bit like a wooden wall safe. I tugged a bit more on the paper, and saw a small keyhole. The key fit into the lock. It turned smoothly, even after all these years.

Yumi came to stand by me as I opened the little wooden door and peered inside with my flashlight. I saw a piece of extremely yellowed paper. I pulled it out, and as I did so, a key dropped to the floor with a delicate ping. I grabbed up the key while looking at the fragile paper.

"Can you read this?"

Yumi took the document and shined her flashlight on it. "It's ... *it's in Japanese!*"

"As I suspected."

"It says ... it's hard to read, it says, where this key fits belongs to the family, Miyake family name." She looked up at me in shock. "Nikki!"

"I know." That was, of course, Yumi's Japanese family name, which her mother had taken back, after her divorce.

Yumi read haltingly a few words, "I have no heirs, but my sister got married and had children. I have been very successful as a milliner to Seattle's women of wealth and style. It was my greatest life's pleasure to do this work, and now I hope my heirs can enjoy some of my success. Whoever you may be, Love from the Past, Miyake Meechie/Meechie Miyake."

"She's written it in both Japanese and American traditions." Yumi was nearly overcome. "Nikki, oh, Nikki. What's happening? How did you … how, I mean … I'm completely confused."

"Let's see if this opens the metal box." I hurried back to it and stuck the key into the keyhole. For the first time in over one-hundred-and-fifty years, the box squeaked opened.

And, even though what I saw was something like what I expected, I couldn't help feeling thunderstruck. The box was filled with stacks of gold coins. And not just any gold coins. *They were antique gold coins.*

"*Oh! Nikki!*" Yumi whispered in shock.

I went into a bit of shock too. I expected something, but this exceeded anything I could imagine.

"What shall we do, Nikki? What shall we do?"

"What we *must* do is get this out of here, directly." I cautiously reached into the hole in the floor—sincerely hoping not to encounter Mr. Mouse or Ms. Rat—to see if there was anything else, but the space was empty. I stood and worked the floorboard back into its place. Then I went to the window, felt around in the space of the wall safe, and again, nothing. I closed and locked the little wooden door, carefully folding the wallpaper back over its outline the best I could.

"This box is too heavy for me to carry by myself. We'll have to put some of the contents in our backpacks, and then, I hope I can handle it. You'll have to hold the flashlight so I can see."

"But Nikki …."

"What?"

"You're … just going to take this?" She waved at the metal box.

"Indeed I am. It's yours. Yours and your mother's. Let's get moving. Hand me your backpack."

"But, doesn't it belong to the person who owns the land?"

"Yumi, let us ponder these questions elsewhere! You read yourself that the contents of this box belong to your family. And, as to it belonging to the person owning the land, that's a very interesting question—does a person owning land own what is under it, which would be worth asking if not for the very document your Great Aunt Meechie left.

"Now, please, give me your backpack!"

Somewhat dazedly, Yumi handed me her backpack and I piled a bunch of the coins into it, then helped her pull it on. Then I did the same with my backpack, while Yumi helped me pull it on. I hefted the metal box. I could handle it. "Okay, let's go!" I flashed the light around the room one more time before handing the flashlight back to Yumi. Everything looked the same as when we entered. I then handed my Dad's toolbox to Yumi and picked up the black metal box.

We walked cautiously through the house, Yumi shining the light through the house, down the porch stairs, back along the boardwalk, and up the dirt steps into daylight. Finally, coming up out of the earth, I strode purposefully to the car.

I looked back at Yumi, who stood at the top of the stairs, both flashlights still on, frozen.

"Come on, Yumi. You have the keys. Turn off the flashlights, come and unlock the car!"

She shook herself as if trying to wake up, then turned off the flashlights, slowly walking toward me.

I glanced around. Of course, no one was here, but still, I felt we must get home, where I would finally feel safe.

"Come on, come on, come on!" I urged, frustrated by her stuck-in-molasses movement.

Finally, she came to the passenger door, put the flashlights down on the ground and dug in her jeans pocket for the keys. Finally! she opened the door.

I took the keys and put the metal box in the trunk with my backpack, then I took Yumi's backpack off her and put it in the trunk as well, closed it and turned to my friend. "Are you okay to drive?"

"I … yes, of course."

She took the keys from me, we climbed into the car, and, at last, were headed home.

Chapter XV
What to do with the Booty?

We said very little on the drive home—pretty much just my saying, "turn right, turn left." I didn't want to distract her from her driving. I had never been so happy to see my big, old, gray, gargoyle-crested apartment building as when it finally loomed into sight.

"We'll only take in our backpacks," I said when we were parked in the parking structure. "I don't know who we might encounter, and I don't want to be carrying that box."

"Okay." Yumi let me help her put on her backpack, then I pulled mine on. We stole inside. I hoped not to see anyone. Not even Homer. Not even Mitch! I wanted to get into the apartment and just—think. I had to think.

We stepped through the door and up to the elevators. Homer was talking with someone in the doorway with his back to us. The elevator pinged and the door slid open. Homer looked over his shoulder at us, and I waved at him, smiling as we stepped into the elevator. Up we went, then down the hall and, at last, into the apartment.

I pulled my backpack off and dropped it on the sofa, then plopped down beside it. Yumi matched me, move by move.

"I don't understand … I don't understand how you knew about this," Yumi said. "I keep replaying in my mind what you did. You just went directly to that house, to that room, to that floorboard … and pried it up, and got that box. How did you do that? How did you know to do that?"

"If I tell you, you won't believe me."

"I'll have to believe you! I have no choice. I saw it. Whatever you say must be the truth. Because it's too … too …."

"Paranormal."

"Yes. Too paranormal. So it has to be paranormal."

"It is."

"Will you tell me?"

"I'll try. Follow me." I got up and went down the hall and into my closet. Yumi followed. I pointed at the mirror. "Things, I mean, people, appear in this mirror. I saw the Millie the Milliner billboard here a few days ago, and then, as I watched, her face shifted to delicate, beautiful features very much, very much like yours. And the letters in the name 'Millie' shifted to 'Meechie' … which is why …."

"Which is why you asked me about that name. And I was surprised, as it happened to be the name of an ancestor."

"Right. Then, after you shared with me your mother's betrayal by her partner, that little gray cat appeared in the mirror this morning and went down the stairs of the underground city, and up into the house where we just were. She went through the house and stood over a bump in the floorboards of the room we were in, and a golden light shone around the floorboard I pulled up.

"I didn't know what it meant, but I knew it was something good. And that it was something for you, from your Victorian aunt."

Yumi looked intently at the mirror, where only she and I were reflected. "I wish it would show me something."

"I don't know if you could see it if it did, Yumi. But I don't think it's likely to show anything now, as the reason for the … visions … has been fulfilled. We can save your mother's business. She needn't try to chase after Ervin. She needn't lose any time trying to regain her finances. Thanks to however many greats your Great Aunt Meechie is, thanks to her, your mother won't miss a moment in her work. Another thing in common between your aunt and your mom is, apparently, creativity."

"Oh! Yes. I see." She bowed her head. "Thank you Aunt Meechie for … for everything!" Then she looked up at me. "But Nikki, now what? I mean, now what do we do?"

I led the way back into the living room and sat down next to my backpack again. "That's what we need to think about. Let's first see what one of these coins might be worth." I pulled a couple of them out of my backpack. "Eighteen-eighty-six twenty dollar gold coin. I guess it's worth more than twenty dollars now! But I have no idea how much." I poked around at the coins in my backpack. "They all seem to be the same, twenty dollar gold coins. What about the ones you have?"

Yumi pulled a few of the coins out of her backpack. "Same. All gold, all stamped with twenty dollars."

I got my laptop and came back to the sofa, pulled up a coin site, and input the information of the coin. And then I thought I'd stop breathing. "Oh!" I whispered.

"What, Nikki, what?"

"I'll say they're worth more than twenty dollars. This one is worth *ten thousand dollars*."

"Ten *thousand*? No."

"Yes. Come look."

She came and sat by me, where I pointed out the value of but one of the hundreds of coins in our possession. "But ... but ... I don't know what to say."

"Say, *'hooray!'* for example."

"Yes. Well. Hooray is inadequate. But, again, do you not think we must tell the owner of the land, or the authorities, or someone?"

"No, I do not think. This fortune belongs to your family, and has come to you by powerful, mystical means. So, first of all, you will not have one cent if you insist on telling anyone. Secondly, you swore to keep Mitch's secret place a secret, so you will be doing harm all over the place if you start tampering with your good fortune. And you will be doing good everywhere if you honor the gift."

Yumi nodded, though somewhat slowly, as if still trying to figure out an argument against my argument. "All right. Apparently, I have to do it your way or be a terrible person."

Not terrible, just unwise."

"Whatever. But here's the next burning question, how do we liquidate them? We'll be faced with the same problem of keeping the secret when we're asked how a couple of young women came upon this fantastic fortune."

"Ummm… yes. Well, we'll just have to liquidate them one or two at a time. And I think that a story close to the truth will suffice. We'll just go to places that buy and sell valuable coins," I waved at my computer, "and tell them that your Aunt passed and left this fortune to the family, which had been handed down through the generations, but now you want to liquidate some of it."

"You'll have to do the talking," Yumi said.

"It's not my aunt."

"I won't be able to … I won't be able to! And, oh, yikes, the problems just keep coming up. You wouldn't think great wealth would have so many problems."

"Now what?"

"My mother! How do we tell my mother? It's all so fantastic and unreal. But, how do I tell my mother? 'Hello Mother, I, um, just happen to have tens of thousands of dollars, and more where that came from. Your problems are over. Don't ask any questions ….'"

Yumi was right. That thought had not yet crossed my mind. It would have, but hadn't yet.

"It seems like we might have to let her in on the whole thing. But …."

"But that's not fair to Mitch," Yumi pointed out. "Were you going to tell Mitch?"

"Well, I think …." The conversation we'd had only yesterday—was it only yesterday?—about telling one another everything, even when difficult, sprung to mind. "I think, yes, of course, I must tell him. He may not believe the paranormal stuff, though."

"I think he will. He'll be like me, left with no alternative."

I put my hand to my chin and my elbow on my knee, thinking hard. Immediately, my phone pinged. It was Mitch. "Jeez, be careful what you think," I warned myself. I answered the phone. "Hi!"

"Hi Nikki, you home? I'm on my way home soon. I have so much to tell you!"

"Yes. I'm home. I kind of have a lot to share, myself."

"Great! See you in a bit. Bye." And he disconnected.

"He's on his way."

"What about Alex?"

"What about Alex?"

"Will it be possible for the three of us to have this huge secret from him?"

"I christen you, '*The Problem Hunter.*' Goodness. Let me catch my breath. And let Mitch make the decision about that."

"Just voicing what comes to mind."

"Yes. It's good, really. Though a bit overwhelming." We sat quietly among our thoughts. A few minutes later, the doorbell rang. We'd stowed the gold coins back in the backpacks. I let him in.

"What a day," he began. "I learned so much. My brain is exploding, but I'm so excited to be an intern at that law firm. Really nice people. Which I didn't necessarily expect. I mean, it's just business, isn't it? But, no, they were very nice to me … and …." He looked from me to Yumi and back to me. "What's going on? You both look like cats who have swallowed canaries."

"Ha!" I said, trying to laugh authentically, but just couldn't. He was right, wasn't he?

"No swallowed canaries, but ... but ...." Oh my goodness, I could not imagine how to continue.

"Nikki is a psychic or a mystic, or something," Yumi blurted out. She reached into her backpack and pulled out a handful of coins. "And she led me to this today, in your underground city. And that, after my mother's partner having embezzled every single penny from the company and disappearing. And Nikki said these coins belong to me. Well, my mother, because my Great Aunt appeared to her.

"And she knew how to find this document." She pulled the flyer from her backpack. "It's in Japanese, old and faded and so hard to read, but, anyway, it says, in short, that this fortune belongs to my family, and that's my mother. Because Millie the Milliner is Meechie, my Great Great Aunt."

It all spilled out like one word, as Mitch stood looking at the coins Yumi had put in his hand.

"*What?*" was all he could utter.

"Heavens! Don't make her say it again," I begged.

"But I don't understand."

"Neither do I, not completely," Yumi said.

"Well, neither do I. Not completely," I added. "I don't know why I have these psychic visions. But I do. And they help people. So, it's good. And I think that's all that matters."

Mitch looked at me with the deepest frown I ever saw. "Psychic visions?"

"Yes. In my mirror."

"That was just my uncle and mother."

"Yes. I mean, no. Not 'just.' The mirror sometimes shows me things. And it showed me the billboard, Millie the Milliner, and then it … morphed to a beautiful Japanese woman, and the letters shifted from 'Millie' to 'Meechie.' I asked Yumi if Meechie was a Japanese name, and she said that it was, and, by coincidence, the name of her Great-Great Aunt. But, as it turns out, not really so much by coincidence."

I continued to tell him the whole story, while he stood looking at the gold coins in his hand. Finally, he sat beside me.

"So last night, when Yumi's mother told her that her partner had stolen every penny from the business account, and, basically, disappeared from the face of the planet …."

"Along with all her patterns and sketches and ideas for the next year …." Yumi added.

"Yes, and that, too, I knew the meaning of the visions. And, to confirm it, I had another vision, where that little gray-striped, green-eyed cat took me right to the very place where I found these coins." I took a deep breath.

"And we've been sitting here, contemplating how to handle everything. How to tell Yumi's mother, and if I should tell you ...."

"You considered not telling me?" Mitch asked, looking at me, shocked.

"I was just sorting everything out. I considered not telling you because it seemed like Yumi's mother's business. But then I remembered our conversation about telling one another everything, and Yumi said that, well, I had to tell you. Which, of course, would have been the only conclusion.

"But Yumi wants to tell everyone. The person who owns the land, the authorities ...."

"That would be pointless and counterproductive," Mitch said. "I'm not a lawyer yet, and I'm glad because I can give you my opinion, without having any clue what the law might say." He shook his head like he didn't believe what he was about to say. "But if things are as you say, and what choice do I have but to believe you, because here's the evidence, then the coins belong to you and your mother, Yumi, it would seem to me. Could I take a look at the document that names your family?"

Yumi handed it to him.

"Oh! It's in Japanese!"

"Yes. As I said," Yumi pointed out.

"That's what makes it even more convincing," I said. "How many milliners named Meechie Miyake do you imagine there were in Seattle around the time of the great fire?"

Mitch's eyebrows raised practically to his hairline. "I would imagine one. Or less."

"Exactly."

"It's all ... all ...."

"I know."

"But, what about Alex?" Yumi insisted.

"I'm surprised you care," I said.

"It just seems like it would be so difficult, I mean, *impossible* to be doing all the stuff we'll have to be doing, without him picking up on the three of us knowing something we're not letting him in on. If it were me, I'd feel very, very bad."

"So would I," I agreed.

"So would I," Mitch said. "I am still processing that you were considering not telling me, Nikki." He looked pointedly at me. "But ... maybe it's something he'd rather not know about. It really has nothing to do with him, but he'll have to keep the secret anyway."

"You could ask him if he wants to know about something that the three of us are dealing with, that he may not wish to know about," I suggested.

"*Weird!*" Yumi said.

"Kind of. But .... everything's weird." I stood up, paced to the window, and looked down into the gathering darkness, into the tops of the trees reaching up, but still, far below—like the answers

I was looking for, all far away. I thought something wonderful had occurred, but the whole situation was fraught with problems!

"I'll … just tell him," Mitch decided. "Or, *we'll* tell him, because, quite frankly, I don't think I *can* tell him, there's too much I don't understand."

"Well, then, invite him over and let's tell him," I said.

Chapter XVI

Alex's Strange & Awesome Uncle

Alex rang the doorbell shortly after Mitch called him. "Hey, Nikki."

"Hey, Alex." We went into the living room.

Alex looked from Yumi to Mitch to me, and read something in our stance, or look, or perhaps just our psychic vibe.

"What's up? You all look like …."

"Please don't say we all look like we swallowed canaries," I begged.

"All right. I wasn't going to say that. But now that you mention it …."

"No swallowing of beautiful little yellow birds. *However!* Unlike you, Yumi and I had an extraordinarily eventful day."

One after the other, or more accurately, one on top of the other, we spilled our jumbled story, while Mitch put the gold coins he held into Alex's hand.

When we sort of began to wind down, Alex held up the coins and asked, "Are these real?"

"Yes, they're real," I answered, incensed.

He smiled, hesitantly. "Is this some sort of a joke?"

I could see now, the very reason we didn't know if we should tell him or not—he might suspect us of playing a stupid trick on him.

"Our jumbled story is real. I found these coins under the floor of the very room you were in the other day in the underground city, when you were all standing at that window where the glass isn't even broken.

"And Yumi's mother was embezzled by her partner. And there is this document with the coins stating that they belong to heirs of the Miyake family, Yumi's family name.

"Now, we have to figure out how to tell Yumi's mother this fantastic story so she'll believe it, and accept the money, and not lose valuable time with the production of her creations."

"Which," Yumi interrupted, "given that that scum-bag Ervin also stole all, *all* of her designs, and erased them from her computer and the cloud, so he can pretend that they're his, I guess, when he surfaces, makes her moving forward, even with money, virtually impossible. But, anyway, the money is good. She can finish producing the current line."

"Yes. The rat, stealing all her designs," I agreed. "Horrible, horrible person. We have to figure out how to liquidate these coins without raising suspicion about where they came from.

"So … if we cannot get you, our closest friend, to believe us, then how will we get to the next step? How will we get Yumi's mother to believe us?"

Alex finally sat down by Yumi. "Okay. I believe you. But, if it has to be so secret, why did you tell me?"

"Do you think we could be running around doing all the stuff we'll have to do," Mitch asked, "without you knowing something was up, and yet, we weren't letting you in on it? We talked about not telling you, because we thought you might prefer not to know. But then, well, I just decided, you need to know."

"And you can use my help," Alex said.

"Well, sure. Any help, in particular, you're thinking of?" I asked.

"My uncle, my mother's brother, is a coin broker. So, I can liquidate these coins." He rattled the coins in his hand. "They're no doubt quite valuable, but I don't think it'll be enough to run a business."

"What about these?" I reached into my backpack and brought up a fistful of coins.

"And these," Yumi said, rattling her heavy backpack.

"*Oh! My!*" Alex exclaimed.

"And roughly as many more in a black metal box in the trunk of my mother's car."

"*Really?!*" Alex and Mitch exclaimed together.

"I suggest you get those into the apartment," Alex said.

"That's our plan. I just didn't want to lug that box inside and perhaps be seen. I plan to go back out this evening, put the box in Dad's backpack, which is bigger than mine, and bring it in."

"Good idea," Alex said softly. "And, I believe I may be able to be helpful in another way, which I'll keep to myself for the moment. But for now, what's your plan to persuade Yumi's mom to come here?"

"Don't know. We have to have some plain old contemporary cash to buy her a ticket to come up. From what Yumi says, her mother really has no money at all."

Alex jumped up. "All right, plan launched. Let's get in motion."

"Going where?" Mitch asked.

"To my uncle. His shop is open for another hour. Let's get moving. But first, Nikki, you need to hide the coins we're not taking. Come along, Mitch, while Nikki and Yumi decide where to stow the goods, let's get my car. We'll meet you out front in fifteen minutes."

"Okay," I said with big, *huge* relief over Alex taking action. And we were not going to tell him? What a mistake that would have been!

*   *

Alex's uncle was a strange, little, hunch-backed man, looking much older than he must be, to be Alex's uncle. I mean, he looked older than anyone's uncle, in the neighborhood of about two-hundred.

When we stepped through the door of his shop, a little bell over the door jangled, and a loud buzzer clanged. The buzzer scared me right out of my skin, I jumped so high. There were video cameras high and low, which I can understand, but the composite effect gave me the creeps.

Alex's uncle greeted him as if he saw him every day, although Alex said he hadn't seen him in two years. And he didn't bat an eyelash—although that was probably because he didn't have any—over the five coins Alex handed him.

Alex didn't bother to introduce us. And I decided to let that be just fine.

"Evaluation?" his uncle asked.

"Cash out," Alex answered.

"Hmmm ...." He screwed a monocle, it looked like right into his eye, and turned each of the coins over. "Nice! Nice, nice. Excellent condition. Let me look." He looked through a gigantic book and scratched some notes as he went.

"Okay, okay, okay ... right. I can only give you about twenty-five K right now. I'll give you that for these three. You take those two back and come later in the week to liquidate them. If that works for you."

Alex looked at Yumi.

"Ah. Yeah," Yumi said, at a loss to say anything else.

Alex's uncle stepped through a beaded curtain, then returned with the largest pile of cash I'd ever seen in real life. He stuffed it in a ginormous envelope, wrote out something on a slip of paper and put that in the envelope too. I assumed it was a receipt of some sort.

"Thanks, Uncle," Alex said.

"Sure thing, kiddo."

We stepped back out into the balmy summer evening, looking at one another like ....where's the cameras, because we must be in a movie.

Alex handed Yumi the envelope. And I don't know why she handed it to me. I stuffed it in my shoulder bag.

"Home. And quickly," I said.

We rode home silently, each sorting our own thoughts. Alex drove into our parking structure and, fortunately, was able to park beside my mom's car. He got a backpack out of his trunk. I saw his intention and unlocked the trunk of Mom's car. He shoved the black box into the backpack, and the four of us slipped into the foyer.

A Homer clone stood at the front door. He saluted us as I pushed the button for the elevator, and I waved. Up we went to the seventh floor. In the apartment, I pulled the envelope from my shoulder bag and handed it to Yumi.

"Why did you hand that to me?"

"I don't know, Nikki. It's all very disconcerting. Real, actual cash. I'm not used to it. I have a card. It has a limit. I have to stay in my limit. Cash, it just feels like, more real. Scary-real." She opened the envelope and the slip of paper fell to the floor. I picked it up and glanced at it.

It was not a receipt. It said, "Which of these beautiful girls is your girlfriend?"

I wanted to chuckle, but ... the funny little man *called me beautiful.* I didn't consider myself even in the same league as Yumi when it came to physical beauty. But … *the funny little man called me beautiful!* I didn't say anything. I just handed the slip of paper to Alex.

He glanced at it, wadded it up and stuck it in his pocket. "None," he said, looking away.

Oh! It made me sad. "Maybe … one day …."

"Doesn't seem likely."

"What?" Yumi asked.

"Nothing," I finally said after a prolonged silence. "Let's move forward with our plan."

As it turned out, it was not that difficult to get Yumi's mother to come up to Seattle. Listening to the one side of the conversation, I heard the tone, if not the words, of Yumi's mother. She was resistant until Yumi said, "It's about great Aunt Meechie, Mother. I have money for a ticket for you to come up, and you need to come up."

There were a few moments of silence on the line. I was tempted to think Yumi's mother had hung up, but then she said something in a very soft tone, and Yumi said, "Yes, Great Aunt Meechie." And then, "What time will you be ready to come? Okay, I'll text you the ticket information."

Then she handed her phone to me. "She wants to write down your address for the Lyft driver."

I gave her my address, and she said, "It will be good to see you, dear."

"It'll be very good to see you too," I said warmly.

I handed the phone back to Yumi. She said her goodbyes then hung up.

"That was too easy," I observed.

"Yes. All I had to do was mention Aunt Meechie."

"I saw that. Interesting. What do you suppose that's about?"

Yumi shrugged. "Family stuff runs deep in Japanese culture. I'm sure my mother knows many things that I will likely never understand. But she's like you. She has second sight."

"Does she?" Perhaps that's why I've always felt a deep, mysterious connection with her. But, why didn't I know that about her? I suppose she protected it, like I tried to protect mine. What others cannot believe in, they often abuse. It's very weird.

"Well, it'll be wonderful to see her," I said. "Plus I don't even have words for how wonderful it will be to share with her this phenomenally good news."

"I can't wait, either." Yumi stood, excited, then sat again. "I'm beside myself."

I laughed. "I see that!"

"So, she's coming tomorrow?" Alex asked.

"Yes," Yumi said, "if I can get a ticket for her. I'd better do that. Excuse me while I go to another room so I can concentrate on getting a reservation."

Alex and Mitch and I stood looking at one another. The Alex sat on the sofa and pulled the black metal box out of his backpack.

"That was good thinking in the parking lot, Alex. Doesn't the box look so Victorian?"

"It does." Alex ran his hand over it. "Amazing story," he sighed. "So, keep me posted about when you want to go back out to my uncle's shop."

"Oh. Yes, I guess we'll be making more than one trip there." Apparently, my odd feelings for the peculiar place and his strange uncle rang in my voice.

"It's probably kind of off-putting," he said. "I'm used to the place, I've gone there on occasion my whole life. Every now and then my mother would find a coin she thought of possible value, and she'd take me with her to his shop. I don't know why only me, among my siblings. But that's what she did. Other times she'd take him a plate of lemon bars. He loves lemon bars."

"Interesting."

"Sarcasm?" Alex asked.

"No! No, not sarcasm. It's just, he's such a strange little man, and it's difficult to imagine him loving lemon bars. If that makes sense."

"Well, he does love them. I've watched him eat an entire plate of lemon bars before my very eyes, without pausing to even see if this bite was as good as the last." Alex stood. "He's 'a funny little man' because he, somehow! survived polio, a disease believed conquered, but he got it, and it bent him up. You should see the pictures of him before then, as a child. He was beautiful. Big eyes, beautiful smile, golden hair in curls. And then, very suddenly, that all changed.

"But I'll grant you, he is a rather odd bird. A good bird. But a strange bird." He headed for the door. "Don't get up, love birds. I shall see you on the morrow, unless you fend me off."

"No fending!" I protested. "We need you, friend bird, more than you need us!" I laughed.

"You ain't seen nothin' yet." And he was out the door.

I turned to Mitch. "What do you suppose he means by that? What is he hinting at, being able to be yet more helpful? I think what he did this evening … well, what more could he do?"

Mitch shrugged. "He's a man of mystery. I'm sure he wouldn't allude to something without there being something."

"Agreed."

"So … if you can tell me, what did that little note say?"

"Oh. It said, 'which of these beautiful girls is your girlfriend.'"

"I see. I wondered at his reaction."

"Yes. Sad. But—*his uncle called me beautiful*. I mean, I'm not even in league with Yumi."

"Oh, will you stop, my dearest. I'm not going to argue about your beauty, which is both external and internal. Just because you're different, doesn't mean you're less."

"No. Of course not. But …."

Yumi came back in the living room. "Done! I got the reservation and texted Mother. She's on an eleven a.m. flight and should be at our door, well, whenever the Seattle traffic from the airport lets her get here. Flight, easy. Traffic, difficult."

"True."

"I'm going to make an almond butter and honey sandwich," Yumi said. "Do you guys want me to some for you, too?"

"Oh! We forgot to eat, I think. Yeah. I'm hungry. Come on Mitch, let's make some sandwiches."

We crowded into the kitchen and bumped into one another, giggling, getting out bread and a variety of nut butters and honey and jams. I made a pot of tea and we sat at the little kitchen booth with our late night supper.

"Alex is pretty amazing," I couldn't help observing aloud.

"Ummm," Yumi responded noncommittally.

"What does 'ummm' actually translate into?"

"Something like, yes-he's-a-nice-guy-for-a-guy."

"He's a nice guy, for a human being. Altogether nice."

"Stop selling him," Yumi warned.

"I'm only saying what I feel. And, look, your mother is coming tomorrow because of him."

"Because of you, first."

"That's true, yes, because of me first, but because of him, second. Or first. Either way, if not for Alex, your mother would not be coming tomorrow."

"Thus, he's nice for a man-type person. And, by the way, I don't count Mitch in my generalities, at all. He's an entirely different sort of being. Human male, yes. And yet, more."

"He's taken!" I laughed.

"Of course," Yumi nodded. "If he wasn't, I wouldn't trust him. You see how that works."

"Yes, I see."

"I'm just the street light," Mitch said. "Hearing everything. Saying nothing. Except I will say, Alex is certainly special, too. Back to being a lamp post." He finished his sandwich and stood. "All right, this lamp post needs to go to bed. I have a feeling tomorrow is going to be a full day."

"Oh! And we never got to talk about your day."

"I wonder why?" He shrugged. "No upstaging around here. Not to worry, my pet. There'll be plenty of time to talk about my experience." He stretched his beautiful body, leaned over and gave me a lingering kiss, and was off to his so-close-and-yet-so-far-away bed.

"You're a lucky girl," Yumi whispered.

"I know." I got up to put my dishes in the dishwasher, only to see all of Mitch's mother's pots and pans. "Whoa! I have to remember to get her cookware to her." I put my dish and silverware in the sink. "I'm off to sleep. Tomorrow comes early. You go to sleep soon, too, all right? You don't want to crash in the middle of the day. Your mother can stay in your room since you're sleeping in the conservatory. I hope she enjoys the posters," I said with an unavoidable edge of sarcasm.

"Oh! That's great!"

"Okay, off I go." I gave Yumi a little hug and was soon in bed. I don't think I was awake for ten minutes, I was that tired.

Chapter XVII

Back Into the Underground City

Just as I had foretold, the next day came early. I had a slew of dreams, none of which I could remember, which is so frustrating, as I like to sort through them to see what my subconscious, who, I'm told, rules the show, actually thinks of things.

And, as I'd had so many "things" happening the previous couple days, I was curious what my subconscious thought. But it was not to be.

I jumped out of bed and started dashing about, when I thought through the fact that Yumi's mother would soon be here, and I had better check out the condition of Yumi's room where her mother would be staying, and the condition of the apartment, in general. But, after a brief inspection, I was pleased that the entire apartment was acceptable for adult scrutiny.

Then I made *myself* "acceptable for adult scrutiny," and finally went to the conservatory. Yumi was on the phone, and, from the sounds of it, her mother was getting into the Lyft at that moment.

"See you soon. Love. Bye." Yumi looked up at

me, all smiles. "She's on her way. I've got to make myself presentable." She leapt up and dashed down the hall.

I tidied up the little rollaway bed, then considered bringing the plants back in from the dining room, but decided against it, as we might have another dinner there, with Yumi's mother joining us. I busied myself watering the plants in the conservatory, and then the plants in the dining room, who seemed, for the moment, to be content to be there, although not in nearly as much light and, of course, away from their peers.

Yumi, looking fresh and adorable as a little garden pansy, came in and watched me water the plants, all jangling with excitement. "Do I look okay?" she asked.

I gave her a teasing critical look, up and down. "Why do you ask? You're always perfect."

"Hardly!"

"Always perfect," I reaffirmed. "Do you want to wait here for her, or would you like to go downstairs and bother Homer until she comes?"

"Let's go bother Homer!"

So down we went to chat with Homer, and catch him up on the fact that Yumi's mother would be staying with us for awhile. It did get a bit tricky when he asked us if there was any special reason she was coming or was she simply inclined to visit?

We both hemmed and hawed awkwardly, which was the same as spilling a big can of beans, it seemed to me. But Yumi finally said something about really wanting to share Seattle with her mother, and, as her fall fashion show was soon, she'd not then be able to come up, so now was the best time.

Every bit of that statement, true! So why did we sound so evasive, Homer must have wondered.

Before long, a Lyft deposited Yumi's beautiful mother at our door. Homer opened the door for her and Yumi introduced them to one another. They were formal and polite. Homer led us to the elevators—despite my knowing where they were!—and gallantly pressed the button.

"Would you like me to bring up your luggage?" he asked, causing me to raise my eyebrows. She had one very small piece of luggage, on wheels.

"No, I can handle it," she replied. "But thank you for your kindness."

Yumi's mother put her arm around Yumi and said something quietly to her that I couldn't hear. There was a soft exchange between them until the elevator door opened.

"How lovely," Yumi's mother said as we stepped into the hall, the soft peachy light and the warm tones of the woodwork and carpet always so cozy and welcoming.

"Would you like some tea?" I asked as we stepped into the apartment.

"That would be lovely, Nikki." She settled on the sofa with Yumi, while I went into the kitchen to make tea, getting out the delicate Japanese tea set for the occasion. It was one of Mom's favorite possessions, and I loved it too. Translucent cranes and a little running stream play on the deftly painted small teacups and teapot. There were even delicate, painted ceramic spoons.

As I brought the tea tray to the coffee table, Yumi came back into the living room and handed her mother the document written in Japanese.

Her mother took the aged document and studied it carefully. She read some of it out loud in the most beautiful, lilting Japanese. I didn't understand a word, of course. But as her mother read, Yumi made little exclamations of surprise.

Finally, her mother looked up from her reading, looking from her daughter to me, and back again. "A wonderful thing has occurred," she said simply.

"Yes. A wonderful thing."

Her mother went on to explain that in the document, Aunt Meechie mentioned several plots of land she'd owned, including, of course, the land that her house was now under.

"If she had no immediate heirs, what became of all that land?" I asked.

Yumi's mother shrugged. "She may have willed it to my grandmother, but I know nothing about that. Otherwise, I suppose, after some time, it simply went to the state."

"Yes. I suppose so. If you would care to follow us, Yumi and I would like to show you what we found."

She nodded, and the three of us went into the guest bedroom. Yumi and I both reached under opposite sides of the bed—neither a safe nor original hiding place—and pulled out our backpacks and the black box, opening them to reveal their contents.

"*Oh, my!*" Yumi's mother sighed, sitting on the edge of the bed, looking overwhelmed. "My, my, my! It's … a fortune."

"It is," I agreed. "A rather large fortune. And you deserve it."

"I deserve it? *You* deserve it," she said to me.

"No. It's not mine. I'm pretty sure good things would not come of my having this fortune."

"How did you …?"

"She has second sight, Mother."

Her mother looked at me thoughtfully and nodded. "Yes. Yes. I remember when you were a little girl and you talked about the angels."

"I did?" I didn't remember that.

"Yes. And you occasionally knew other things, that I suspected were paranormal."

"She sees things in a mirror," Yumi went on.

I wasn't sure I wanted that shared. But there it was.

"Scrying," her mother said.

"Scrying? It's … a real thing?"

"To people like the two of us, it's very real. To most people, it's utter nonsense. Thus, we must protect our gift and be careful about who we share it with."

"Well, despite how close I am with my parents, you and Yumi are the only people who know about it. And you heard me tell Mitch about it."

"Yes. He's still doubtful." Yumi acknowledged.

I realized then, of course, I must share my mirror with Yumi's mother. "Let's stow the coins back into their admittedly very poor hiding place, and I'll show you my mirror."

When we crowded into my closet, I flipped on the light, and there we stood, most unremarkably, in front of the mirror.

"I only see things when it's almost dark," I said, flipping the light off. "And even then, it's quite rare. I mean, I never look for anything. It just … appears."

We stood watching, but nothing materialized.

"Well, Nikki, I don't imagine anything will appear now, as this scrying surface is for your eyes only."

We stepped back into my bedroom and Yumi's mother looked around. "Very charming, dear. Such a lovely room. And," much to my surprise, she gave me a hug, "I noticed the posters of anime artists on the walls of the guest bedroom, which, obviously, you very thoughtfully bought for my Yumi."

I nodded, a bit overcome with a wave of emotion.

"She's very special," Yumi said, "our Nikki."

"She certainly is!"

"Oh! You'll make me cry!"

They both giggled as if I'd said something very funny. I have to admit that I sometimes completely do not understand the Japanese funny bone. Yumi and her mother had been in my life for most of my life, but there were still times when the two of them would fall into a giggle fest that I had no idea what was funny.

"What would you like to do now?" I asked. "What do you think is the best way to move forward?"

"Well, I'm not sure," Yumi's mother said. "All the events of the last few days, Ervin stealing everything from me, and this miracle on the heels of it—I've not had time to think, to process. But what I would like to do ….” She hesitated.

“Yes? Please, say anything.”

“I’d like to see my great aunt’s house. I’d very much like to be in the space where you found the coins.”

I could not very well say no. But it was for Mitch to say “yes.” “Let me talk with Mitch. Excuse me.” I stepped back into my bedroom where I’d left my phone, and gave him a thumbnail sketch of the previous few minutes, and Yumi’s mother’s request. He paused, but quietly agreed to take us to his underground city.

“And Alex, too?” I asked. I had an ulterior motive, which, for the moment, I would keep to myself.

“Well, sure, why not?”

*   *

After suggesting to Yumi’s mother that she get into more rough-and-tumble clothing, resulting in her changing into a pair of Yumi’s jeans, tee-shirt, and shoes, as she had not brought any such clothes with her, the five of us piled into Mitch’s car, and were soon on the road, enjoying yet another sunny day. There was little conversation, other than a chat between Alex and Yumi’s mother about his uncle, with information regarding liquidating the coins.

I didn’t pay much attention to their conversation, considering it to be none of my business. Also, I was preoccupied with wondering what Yumi’s mother would think of the experience she was about to have. If she also had "second sight," it could be quite intense.

We soon came to our, now familiar, hillside. After Mitch parked the car we got out our flashlights, and Mitch led the way, descending down the dirt stairs. Yumi, her mother, and I paused on the stairs, taking in Millie's billboard. She did not transform. No need to now, but I never tired of looking at her.

Just, never.

Finally, we continued on down into the underground city, joining Mitch and Alex.

"*Amazing!*" Yumi's mother whispered, looking about in wonder at the houses, the boardwalk, the entire environment.

We came to what we now knew to be "Aunt Meechie's House" and went up the porch steps, through the front door, passing through the front two rooms and coming to the third room.

"*Oh!*" Yumi's mother exclaimed softly. "*Yes!*" She moved around the room, our flashlights shining a path as she moved. The effect of the moving light path and her delicate footfalls was mystical and beautiful.

She moved her hands through the air as if touching something. I could see nothing, but she obviously interacted with something from an era long, long, gone by. I almost suspected the spirit of Aunt Meechie was in her at the moment.

She moved to the back wall and pressed on some nearly invisible lever, and we all gasped and jumped when a section of the wall slid up into the ceiling. Before us were revealed *hats!*

Breathtaking hats of the Victorian Era, in pristine, perfect condition. That's when I noticed glass on the back side of the opening and realized that I was probably looking at the display that would be seen from the street side.

Wow-oh-wow! Incredible!

She moved further along the wall and pressed another lever, and again, a section of the wall scrolled up into the ceiling. Unbelievable that, after a century-and-a-half, the mechanism worked perfectly. There, more absolutely incomparable hats were revealed.

Yumi, trance-like, moved to the hats. She reached out to touch one, and I had a very, very strong sense that she must not touch it.

"*No!*" I exclaimed as her hand came in contact with the gigantic purple hat, all covered in netting and feathers and flowers.

The hat instantaneously crumbled to dust as Yumi's fingers barely came in contact with it.

"*Ohhhhh!*" we all sighed, in shock.

"Oh, no," Yumi cried. "What have I done? *What have I done?*"

I went to her and put my arm around her shoulders. "It's all right. I mean, you have to be okay with what happened. We all saw the hat. The picture of it is in our memory. Just like all of them, which cannot be touched. There's no way to preserve them but to leave them."

"And hope, when the wall is brought back down, the vibration doesn't destroy them," Alex observed.

"They withstood the wall scrolling up," I said. "Hopefully, when it comes back down, it won't harm them. I think it was being touched that the hat couldn't survive."

"I feel terrible," Yumi said.

"Don't," Alex and I said together.

"But you knew not to touch it," Yumi said to me. "You exclaimed, but it was too late!"

"Yes, something in me knew that they must not be touched. Not anything I would know on my own, I assure you." I looked over at Yumi's mother, wondering why she had nothing to say about the event. She stood at the opposite end of the hat display, her stare fixed beyond the hats, and I knew she was looking out into the street, into another time.

Yumi followed my gaze. "Mother?" She turned to me. "She doesn't seem to be present," she said anxiously.

"No. She doesn't. I think she may be channeling Great Aunt Meechie."

"Oh! Is she all right?"

"I'm sure she is. I believe we must not shock her, but let her return of her own accord."

The four of us huddled together while Yumi's mother appeared to enjoy the sights she saw. She smiled softly. And then, after a few minutes, she pushed first one lever to close the wall upon the hats, and then the other.

As we watched the walls slide down, we did not see any of the hats disintegrate, for which I was extremely thankful, as I knew it would upset Yumi so very much. When the second wall had clicked into place, Yumi's mother shivered, and I saw a faint image of a woman in Victorian clothing pass from her and dissipate into the air.

Great Aunt Meechie.

Yumi's mother turned to us. "Thank you for bringing me here. I'm ready to go, now."

We all silently walked back through the house, down the porch steps, onto the boardwalk, and, finally up the dirt steps, pausing, as always, to give "Millie" a moment's meditation, before stepping back out into the bright sunlight.

"Do you happen to know who owns this land?" Yumi's mother asked Mitch.

"Yes, I do. He lives over there." He gestured.

"Do you mind taking me there."

"Wel-l-l-l, I guess I can't mind. But I hope you're not going to tell him about my discovery."

"Oh, most decidedly not!" she answered emphatically. "I just have a couple questions for him, which will have nothing to do with your underground city. Well, that's not quite truthful. But he'll have no idea that my questions have to do with the underground city because he doesn't know it exists. But I do have a couple urgent questions."

Mitch sighed, but it seemed he had no alternative. Anyone could find out the owner of the property in a few minutes on the web. Mitch and I exchanged a glance in which I said, "trust her," and his look replied, "I have no choice."

A few minutes later, Mitch pulled up on the street in front of a big, old farmhouse. There were smaller, contemporary houses all around it. It was clear that this farmhouse had been here long before the others.

"I'll be back soon."

We watched as Yumi's mother walked to the house and knocked on the front door. A man opened it, and, a bit to my surprise, let her in.

This did not make me comfortable. She just walked into a house with someone no one knew anything about. But I didn't voice my discomfort, not wanting to cause alarm where perhaps none was called for. The moments ticked slowly by while we waited and waited for her to return. Finally, she stepped out the front door, and, smiling warmly, she shook the man's hand, then hurried back to the car.

"I now own two acres of this man's land, where your underground city is, Mitch, and a bit more beyond that. Where, I guess, there may be more underground city. All we have to do is draw up some paperwork, easy enough. I offered him a price that made his eyebrows practically fly off his face.

"He said that it was more than fair, and he had no particular use for that bit of land, as it was at the end of his property, and he really never did anything with it. He did ask why I was interested in it, and I told him the truth. That it had belonged to my great aunt, and I wanted it back in the family." Her elation was contagious, and we babbled like a tree full of crows all the way home.

Chapter XVIII
Love Over Money

When we got back to the apartment, the four of us made Yumi's mother sit in the living room while we bumped into one another in the kitchen making a meal out of whatever we could find.

I was still blown away by what had transpired. The underground city was now safe! Yumi's mother would own it, free and clear, in a few days. Looking at Mitch, I saw a smile on his face like almost nothing I'd ever seen before. It made my heart ring like a bell.

Leaning over, I whispered in Yumi's ear, "Really loving your mother right now."

"Yeah. She's super-mother."

Soon we brought our strange meal of bread and nut butters and a couple cans of beans heated up, and a salad to the coffee table. No actual construction of a recognizable dish was engaged in. We sat around the coffee table, inhaling the weird meal.

"Sorry," I apologized to Yumi's mother, "this isn't a real meal, but we'll have one eventually, I promise."

"It's good to just let go and be casual on occasion," she said.

I don't think I've ever heard her say anything like that! But I was grateful for her playing along. She made a lovely almond butter sandwich with lettuce, and I followed her lead.

"So, here are some of my thoughts," she continued. "I believe, Mitch, you will continue to be interested in the underground city, am I right?"

"Yes. Adamantly, yes."

"So I appoint you overseer and protector of the underground city. It is for you to attend to it the best you see fit. And then, if you still feel this way in the future, when you're twenty-one, I will sign the deed over to you, giving you the property, free and clear."

Mitch dropped his fork, and we all stared at her, speechless. Finally, Mitch said, "I don't know what to say, Mrs. Miyake. Thank you! Thank you! But— that property means so much to you, are you sure you want to give it to me?"

"Yes. There'll be a codicil in the paperwork that Yumi and I get to visit the site as we please, which I'm sure you won't mind."

"Of course not."

"Then we're good?" She reached across to shake Mitch's hand.

He shook her hand enthusiastically. *"We're very good!"*

As we munched away on our weird meal, I finally gathered the courage to ask my question that would not go away. "Mika-san," I said, adding the term of respect to her first name, "were you channeling Aunt Meechie?"

"Could you tell?"

"Well, Mama-san," Yumi said, "something was going on. You were not present."

"No. I wasn't. It's a little vague to me, but yes, I was channeling Aunt Meechie. I recall looking out the front windows through her hats and seeing the street. It was gorgeous! The horses and carts, everyone dressed up beautifully—women in long dresses, men in top hats. Very formal. But everyone comfortable and contented, going about their business.

"And then, I felt her leave me."

"Yes," I said.

"Did you see something?"

"Yes. I saw a woman like a mist leave your body and dissipate into nothing."

"You did?" Yumi exclaimed. "And you didn't tell me?"

"Well … I didn't know but that maybe you saw her too."

"No. I didn't." She sounded very disappointed.

"Don't worry, dear," her mother said. "Second sight can be just as much a curse as a blessing."

"True," I agreed. Everyone looked at me, but I had nothing further to say on the subject. It was too hard to try to explain how odd it was to see and know things that the people closest to you could neither see nor know. Yumi's mother caught my glance, and I saw she knew exactly what I meant, and why I remained silent.

"What's important," Mitch said, filling in the awkward silence, "is that this turn of events has saved your business."

"I hope," Yumi's mother said. "I will still take a big hit in trying to regenerate my spring line. My ideas come through me in a flow. And now with every single one of my designs gone, I feel overwhelmed. I really don't know how I'll regenerate some of those ideas, far too many of them I can't even recall. I think it's due to the shock of what Ervin has done. I'm hoping, that with this financial security, I'll feel calm enough to be able to regenerate some of those creations.

"He even went into the cloud and destroyed everything I had there. I have some older hard drives with older seasonal design lines on them. But they're of little value when what I need is the current line, and forward."

"And this is where I hope to be able to help," Alex said.

"How so, Alex?" I asked.

"I have certain computer hacking skills that might prove useful."

"You? Hacking skills? Why would that be? You're one of the most honest people I know. Why would you be hacking?"

"Well, a couple years ago someone did to my father's business something like what has happened here. My dad lost a small fortune to someone he very much trusted. And I decided the best way to fight fire was with fire. I studied hacking up one side and down the other, took all the info Dad had on this horrible person, and succeeded in taking everything back. And I wiped his system clean. He had no recourse but to slink off with his tail between his legs, like the rat he was. No insult to rats intended."

We looked at him, dumbfounded.

I finally pulled myself out of shock. "Let's get at it! What do you need?"

"I need every single bit of computer info you can give me on this Ervin guy," he said to Yumi's mom. "And I need to see what's the most powerful computer you have here, Nikki. If you don't have one powerful enough, I may have to go home."

"My dad's computer is in their room. I think it might serve your needs because he works on it all the time, and does some pretty high level, complicated computer stuff for his company. Let's go see." We stood and made our way down the hall to my parent's room. I opened the door and then felt immediately very odd, like this was wrong to go into their space without their knowing it.

But the challenge at hand was considerably more important, and I decided I would address the other concern at another time. We stepped into their room, which looked like it came out of an ad for bedding or some-such.

I gestured to the huge and conspicuous computer in the corner of the room.

"*Awesome!*" Alex said, going to it and flipping it on as if it was his very own computer. "Okay, Mrs. Miyake, please come and sit by me, and let's see what we can do to make things right. I hope you have details of this Ervin person with you."

"Oh, yes, everything of mine was on his system and everything—that I know of, anyway—of his I have on my system. Good thing I brought my laptop. I'll get it and be right back."

Soon the two of them were side by side, Yumi's mother giving Alex information that Alex adroitly input.

"We'll leave you two to it," I said, gesturing to Mitch and Yumi to follow me and leave them to their counterspy tactics. We went back to the living room, plopping ourselves down on the sofas, looking at each other in bemusement.

"What we did not know about our sweet, little Alex!" I exclaimed. "Did you know he was a computer genius, Mitch?"

"I had no clue. He's not said a word."

"And I go to school with him! We're in a couple classes together, and also—no clue!"

"He … he's going to try to help my mother recover her precious designs. I … I'm … I feel confused! He's a boy, but he keeps just being … *so nice!*"

"I told you there are young men who are more than nice. They are *wonderful.*" I leaned into Mitch, who sat as close to me as he could. *So yummy!*

"If he's able to retrieve Mother's designs, he'll be more than wonderful. He'll be a miracle worker.

My mother's designs are inspired. I've seen her sketch out a clothing line on the computer in twenty-four hours, working non-stop around the clock. And when it's done, it's done. She turns off the computer, and won't look at it for a couple of days. Then she'll turn it back on, and critique the original ideas. But they're flawless!

"I've asked her to tell me where those designs come from, and she says she has no idea. It's her genius. It takes over, and she is … like she was this afternoon when she channeled Aunt Meechie.

"This is what happened with her fall line. She did the original creation, locked the designs away, Ervin came in and stole it. He knows, too, this is how she creates. He knew that if he stole her line before she made up any of the designs, she would not be able to regenerate it, and he'd have it as if it was his.

"If Alex can get her work back I will have such different feelings about him."

"And if he can't reclaim her work …?" I asked.

Yumi looked at me. "Whether he's successful or not, he's still the same person who has an intention of helping my mother, because he's a good, and kind, and caring person," Yumi said softly.

"That's right," I nodded, very pleased that she said it out loud. "But we still hope for the best, and that justice is done!"

For the next several hours we hardly moved, no one able to go to bed, though the three of us took catnaps on the sofas. Every now and then we'd hear a slightly raised voice from my parents' room, and we hoped it would lead to their declaration of success, but it never came.

As time wore on, I feared triumph was not to be had.

Finally, the sun began to make a weak appearance through the windows of the living room, faint sparkles of sun rays playing on the baby grand piano's keys. I sat in the corner of the sofa, Mitch stretched out sleeping, his head in my lap. I was enjoying the sun's soundless music on the piano keys, when an eruption of cheers came from my parents' bedroom. The three of us leapt up and ran into the bedroom.

I couldn't have been more surprised by any sight than to see Alex and Yumi's mother actually waltzing around the bedroom, Alex humming something indistinctly.

I'm quite certain I've *never* seen Yumi's mother do anything so nearly ridiculous and spontaneous.

"Did you do it? Did you do it?" I shouted over his noisy music.

Alex stopped and waved at the computer screen. There were sketches of a stunning clothing line, unlike anything I'd ever seen. "Oh! Look at those! No wonder he wanted to steal them. They're amazing!

"Did you take them off his system?"

"Yes, dear Nikki, I wiped his hard drive clean. he won't even know what caused it. He can just think it's karma. Which, of course, it is!"

*   *

It took a while until everyone settled down a bit, which did not occur before Mitch had taken me in his arms to dance around the bedroom too, and Yumi's mother handed Alex off to dance with Yumi. Looking at her, I saw she let herself enjoy it!

We finally all trooped into the kitchen for some cold cereal and hot tea. Everyone incredibly tired. Incredibly cheerful. Incredibly giddy. When we were settled in the little breakfast booth, I stood at the end, hovering over them, pleased as ever I had been in my life.

"I don't know how to repay you," Yumi's mother said to me.

"Repay me? There's nothing to repay. Your happiness and Yumi's happiness are my happiness. And you now own Mitch's underground city, which is very important to him, and, well, that's so much more than I could ever have imagined. I did nothing! Energy or information or, whatever it is came through me, and I shared it. But I, Nikki Francis, did nothing!"

"*OHHHHHH!*" they all exclaimed, in huge and unified disagreement. And then they made me shy as they all talked over one another, regaling me with their thoughts of how wonderful I am.

Moments like that are what life is made of. Money is as nothing next to such candid love.

"Despite your protest, Nikki, I want to give you something. I want to give you your choice of whatever you would like from my new line, which your friend has saved."

Shocked, I put down my bowl of cereal. "Oh, no, that's too much!"

"No. It's not enough. But I offer it, anyway."

"But … I'm not … I'm not sophisticated enough to wear your amazing designs."

"Phooey!" she erupted in a most unlike Mrs. Miyake way. "You do not see yourself."

"As I keep telling her," Mitch added.

I thought about how Mom occasionally got one of Yumi's mother's 'little black dresses,' and they were my favorites among all her beautiful—and sophisticated!—clothes.

"I have always loved everything you create. But, most especially, 'the little black dress' that you come up with in every line, that is always so simple, but always different and beautiful."

"Excellent taste, just like your mother. You will have, my dear, the first little black dress of next year's spring line."

My three friends cheered madly, as if I'd just crossed the finish line in a triathlon, or something.

I felt immeasurably shy, but—*happy!*

Chapter XIX
Emerald Eyes

The next day, Alex took Yumi's mother around, liquidating as many of the coins as she needed for the time being, which, of course, was not all of them, not by a long way. Then they put most of what was left in a bank lockbox. She took a few with her, but, for good reason, didn't want them on her person.

She then had to hurry back to Southern California to attend to business. Mitch insisted on driving her to the airport, and I was glad that he did because we all wanted to go to the airport with her. The four of us waved good-bye as she went through security. And then, as we walked back to the car, to my shock and delight, I looked back and saw Yumi reach out and take Alex's hand! I would never have believed it if I hadn't seen it with my own eyes!

I nudged Mitch to look back at them. He took in their hand-holding, Alex, with a completely goofy grin on his face. "My goodness," Mitch whispered to me, "he finally screwed up some courage!"

"Not he," I whispered back. "*She!*"

"*Really?*"

The two of us grinned with our own goofy grins, all the way to the car.

What a fantastic summer, and it's only just begun!

*   *

That night, after everything had settled down, and Yumi was deep in the depths of her dreams, I closed my bedroom door and pulled out my Grammy's emerald ring from its hiding place. It was long past time to share some of what I'd been experiencing. To be sure of my privacy, I went into my closet and sat on the floor, closing the door to just a crack. Thinking about Grammy, I wondered what she might say to all that I'd experienced the last few days.

As I held the ring and thought about the amazing experiences, I saw movement in the mirror. I took my gaze from the ring to the mirror.

And there sat that little gray-striped cat. She looked up at me, her emerald green eyes holding my gaze.

Oh! Now I understood! The little cat was a familiar, *a gift from Grammy!* Holding Grammy's emerald ring close, I shared with the little cat everything I held in my heart, just like I always had with Grammy.

THE END

Hello Dear Reader!

I hope you enjoyed
Millie in the Mirror.

For some more fun, here's *Chapter 1* of Nikki's next adventure:
The Angel in the Mirror

Chapter 1

Two Roads Diverged in a Wood

Yumi and I sat cozily at the little kitchen nook table. I was waiting for a call from Mitch, who was getting his old Chevy a much-needed tune-up. As soon as he got back, the plan was he'd pick up Alex, then call me and Yumi and we'd scurry down to the front door. Off we'd go for a day's exploration of the underground city.

Right then my phone pinged. I was surprised to see it wasn't Mitch. It was Dad. "Good morning my little hummingbird. How's it going?"

"Going great, Dad. What's up?"

"Well, I'm just sitting here in the O.C. airport waiting to go to a meeting in Victoria, B.C., which isn't until tomorrow. And then it dawned on me, as I have a connection in Seattle, I could take a later flight and you could come to the airport and we could have lunch together!" His tone had risen half-an-octave in his enthusiasm.

My eyebrows went straight up into my bangs. "Lunch at SeaTac today?"

Yumi's shocked expression matched mine.

"Sure! Spontaneous fun, right?"

"Ahm. But, Dad … I'd love to see you and all, but not only will it take me as long to get to the airport—spontaneously—as it will take you to get there from Orange County ... I … I have plans for the day."

There was a pause. "You can't change your plans for your dear old dad?"

I felt like a criminal, hearing his hurt tone of voice. "I could, Dad. But it's not just my plans, it's three other people's plans, too. And, again, I'd have to get to the airport …."

"Right. Oh, of course, other people's plans. And getting to the airport." He paused again. "I didn't really think it through, did I?" His voice sounded a bit more chipper. "Well, you know, your dad means well, even when he misfires."

I started feeling unpleasantly, darkly worse. I'm an ogre, I'm a terrible person. Would it truly be so impossible to change everyone's plans and get to the airport? I started to waffle when Mitch's call came in. "Hang on a sec, Dad. Mitch is calling."

"That's okay, sweetie. I'll ring off now. Have a great day." He hung up.

I connected with Mitch.

"Ready to go? We're out front."

"Ah, right. We'll be right down." I clicked off.

"You should see your face, Nikki," Yumi said.

"I'm a terrible person." I got up and headed for my bedroom to get my backpack. "A terrible, terrible person," I muttered down the hall.

I stepped into my closet to grab a jacket, and right then, the mirror started stirring and roiling.

"Now?" I whispered, wanting, rather, to yell. "You're going to demand my attention right now? Don't I have enough to deal with?"

But I couldn't not watch, and as I did, the sepia stirring started to take shape—a large, high-ceilinged room, dark walnut wainscoting, and rows of long walnut tables, with little dark green lights on them, with accompanying walnut chairs neatly lined up at the tables.

Except for one chair, where a man sat hunched over a huge book or newspaper—I couldn't quite make it out.

"It's a library," I said softly.

But—why was I seeing this? Who was this man?

As if in response to my thought, the vision slowly moved around to his side. I couldn't believe it. It looked like—it looked like Homer, our beloved doorman.

What could that mean?

"Are you coming, Nikki?" Yumi asked, coming into my room. "They're waiting for us. I just got a call from Alex."

The vision quickly faded. "Yeah. Sorry. Couldn't find my jacket," I white-lied, coming out of my closet, jacket in hand. "Let's … go."

Yumi gave me a really hard look. "You look … strange."

"I am strange! Come on!"

I grabbed my backpack and we hurried down to the front door, where Homer, all smiles as always, held the door open for us. "Your carriage awaits, young ladies!"

"Thank you, Homer," we said in unison.

But I couldn't help giving him a studied glance. Why-oh-why had he just appeared in a vision in my scrying mirror?

As we hurried out to the car, Alex jumped out of the front seat, and opened the back door, while Yumi got in the back and I joined Mitch in the front. Doors clanged shut and we all waved to Homer as we took off.

"Got the old jalopy tuned-up and ready for more adventure," Mitch said, as he made his way into the traffic.

"Right," I said softly.

He glanced over at me. "What's ...."

"She's feeling terrible because her dad just called and said he'd be at SeaTac this afternoon on his way to Victoria, and she should come out to the airport and have lunch with him," Yumi offered from the back seat. "She told him she had plans."

"I'm a terrible person," I reiterated.

"Oh, Nikki! You should have lunch with your dad," Mitch said. "We can explore any time."

"Well, yes. But, spontaneously like that, I couldn't see changing everyone's plans, just because he couldn't plan a bit himself. If Mom had been with him she would have put a stop to it before his phone finished dialing my number. He didn't mean it bad. But it's as if I'm a house plant, sitting on a shelf, waiting for his sunshine, or something."

"Ah! Guilt brings out the poet in you."

"Hmmmm." I looked out the side window at the storefronts passing by, thinking about how much I'd been looking forward to this very day, just to have some fun and not have to take care of anything, the four of us exploring the underground city.

I'd gone through a lot the last few days—helping Yumi's mother tie-up her business of turning the gold antique coins into modern-day cash, then getting her to the airport.

And, finally, making the adjustment back home, with just Yumi and me there—at last!

The view out the window began to shift to fewer houses and more open terrain. I sighed deeply. This is what I needed! Some open space, some sunshine, and some silly no-agenda banter with my best friends.

But Dad! I hadn't seen him in weeks, and it was so sweet that he wanted to spend time with me. Not every girl had a father who doted on her. My own best friend in the back seat hadn't had her father in her life since she was five.

Urg! All that, and furthermore! I had to contemplate the vision of Homer in the mirror. There was too much to think about. Would it be asking too much to simply let my brain be empty for a while? I wanted not to have to think about anything. I needed a white-noise-mind-noise-cancelling space.

The terrain around us had become even more open with more green rolling hills than houses. The sunlight and green vista let me release my anxiety and circling thoughts yet more, and I sighed deeply.

"Goodness!" Mitch said. "You let go of something!"

"Oh! Sorry!" I smiled at him, sheepishly.

"Nothing to apologize for! You've had a lot to deal with, and now your Dad adds to it. I think it all merits several large sighs."

"Probably. But I think I'll reserve the others for later," I giggled. We pulled onto the grassy hillside under which the Victorian underground Seattle lay sleeping. "Oh, boy, here we are!" I exclaimed.

We piled out and gathered our flashlights and backpacks. Mitch led the way down the dirt steps into the bowels of the earth. But we all paused on the four steps around the antique poster of Millie the Milliner, silently paying a few moments of homage to Yumi's several-Greats Aunt, who had reached out from the past and saved her great-great, darling, nieces.

Then we continued down into the darkness-of-darkness, which always, strangely, became so much lighter, once we'd been there for a while.

When we were all on the boardwalk, Mitch asked, "Do we want to explore a house we haven't gone into yet, or do we want to continue farther than we've gone before?"

"I'd kinda like to see the inside of the houses near Aunt Meechie's," Yumi said.

Both Mitch and Alex made vague noises in agreement.

But I felt something well up in me that I could not stop. "I want to continue on. I … I feel like I really have to see something further on." Wow! Where was this coming from? I mean, why did I care? I just wanted to hang out with my friends. Any exploration we did should be fine with me. But it wasn't.

"Well, that's okay too," Yumi said in her soft, sweet voice. "The houses are probably not going anywhere. We can explore them some other time."

It was dark, but I could feel them all looking at me like, "What's up with Nikki?"

"Sorry." There I was, apologizing again! "I just … just sort of feel like there's something I'll see that I … need to see."

"Let's do it!" Alex said diplomatically.

I have the best friends in the whole entire world! Every one of them takes my weirdness in stride.

Off we went into the darkness, our flashlights weaving a path on the boardwalk, with Mitch leading the way. Even though we could walk two-abreast, we'd agreed to walk single file, just in case we encountered anything unanticipated—like the boardwalk suddenly gone, or whatever.

We made fairly quick progress along the path we were familiar with, but before long, we found ourselves in new territory. Or at least it was for Alex and Yumi.

"Oh, look at that house. I haven't seen it before," Yumi exclaimed.

"Me neither," Alex said, as we stopped before a particularly large, ornate, Victorian house.

"I've seen it," I said, remembering the time I went looking for Mitch when we were in the throes of sorting out our relationship. Goodness, that seemed like a long, long time ago!

"Oh, right. That night," Mitch said softly.

"That night," I nodded. He and I exchanged a look. Our relationship had grown to a whole new level that night. "Let's continue," I urged. There was something I had to see. I didn't know what it was, but it called to me, just the same.

So we continued on, saying little, cautioning one another to be careful when the boardwalk became a bit wobbly for a span. But then it felt sturdy underfoot again.

Now we'd gone farther than I'd ever been, and it had become ever darker. I could barely see Mitch's shoes in front of me. "Have you been this far before?" I asked him.

"Yes, and farther still. There's a 'Y' up ahead on the path."

We fell into a silent lock-step, and sure enough, before long, the boardwalk came to a 'Y.'

We stood in a tight bunch at the 'Y,' flashlights playing on the walls around us.

"Two roads diverged in a wood, and I –
I took the one less traveled by"
Alex quoted.

"Beautiful," Yumi whispered.

"Very beautiful," I agreed. "But I'm pretty sure both of these roads have been 'much less traveled by' for a very, very, long time. Not counting Mitch, of course. Which path did you take? We'll go the other way so it's new for you, too."

"I went right," he gestured with his flashlight.

"Left it is!" I said.

Mitch turned and led the way down a road that, I felt certain, would make all the difference....

About Thea ....

I live in the greater Portland, Oregon area. I love the Great Northwest where the rainy weather, lush green territory, waterfalls, mountains, charming neighborhoods, the Pacific ocean nearby, and a strong writing community—all contributing to making my writing life a dream come true.

You can write to me at:

Thea@EmersonandTilman.com

Have a Happy Day!
Thea

About Blythe ....

I live in a forest with a few domestic and numerous wild creatures, where I create an ever-growing inventory of books and short stories, with a bit of wood carving when I need a change of pace.

All the creatures in my forest and I are glad you "stopped by." If you enjoyed *Millie in the Mirror,* I hope you'll share it with others.

If you'd like to write me, I'd be happy to hear from you!

Blythe@BlytheAyne.com

www.BlytheAyne.com

'Til We Meet Again!
Blythe

Thank you ....

For reading Nikki's story, ***Millie in the Mirror***.

Nikki has continuing adventures in ***The Angel in the Mirror***, where she, Mitch, and her close friends, Yumi and Alex continue to explore Seattle's mysterious *Underground City*, and the paranormal fun and romance advance to a whole new level.

Is there a story you'd like to read about Nikki's adventures? We'd love to hear about it!

If you've enjoyed Nikki's story perhaps you'd write a review as readers are interested in what other readers have to say about a story. And we love to know what our readers have to say!

Until Next Time,

Thea Thomas

&

Blythe Ayne